To My
Ex-Husband

To My Ex-Husband

Susan Dundon

WILLIAM MORROW AND COMPANY, INC.
NEW YORK

Dialogue from the motion picture *Patti Rocks* is reprinted by permission of David Burton Morris.

It is the policy of William Morrow and Company, Inc., and its imprints and affiliates, recognizing the importance of preserving what has been written, to print the books we publish on acid-free paper, and we exert our best efforts to that end.

Library of Congress Cataloging-in-Publication Data

Dundon, Susan.
   To my ex-husband / Susan Dundon.
      p.   cm.
   ISBN 0-688-12459-3
      1. Divorced women—United States—Fiction.   2. Marriage—United
States—Fiction.   I. Title.
   PS3554.U4657T6   1994
   813'.54—dc20   93-27124
                                                              CIP

Printed in the United States of America

First Edition

1 2 3 4 5 6 7 8 9 10

BOOK DESIGN BY BARBARA COHEN ARONICA

For Geoffrey and Cydney
and
For Jennifer and Rachael who came later

A C K N O W L E D G M E N T S

I would like to thank the Virginia Center for the Creative Arts for its generous support.

1989

The other night I walked up the road to the house where you and the children and I used to stay in the summer. There was a nearly full moon and the stars were out. So much light gave the house an eerie, one-dimensional aspect, like a stage set. I stole up the driveway and saw the new tenants through the window of the sun porch, their shoulders hunched over fans of playing cards.

Beyond them, in the living room, I saw all of us— you, me, Annie, and Peter, just as we used to be on those cold, foggy evenings in front of the fire, engrossed in our own game of Go Fish. It was all so clear, Peter in his habitual baseball cap, and Annie, with those strawberry wisps that she was forever letting grow pinned back by about eight barrettes. My throat ached. How I wanted to go in, sit down with my family, and take up my cards, as though I'd just returned from the kitchen with more coffee. How I wanted, if only for a few moments, for the years to fall away so we could be back there as we were.

I can't say how long I lingered. But suddenly someone appeared at the door, and I spun around and ran, bounding breathlessly behind my shadow like a thief.

I was getting married the next day. I know. You're thinking, "How bizarre." What a way to spend the night before your wedding. But perhaps that visit served a purpose, a ceremonial crossing from one life into another.

I always thought that when people got married a second time there was this great divide, that a curtain came down over the past and there you were, neatly contained in the present. Unfortunately, it isn't like that at all, but messier, everything running together in this awful river of confusion. Events carry me along, while every now and then my memory catches on something, such as the night Peter was born, and I'm trapped, like a clump of leaves that can't work its way back into the mainstream. Maybe it's just me. Maybe I'm one of those people who's haunted by history, who will never be truly released from it.

I'm like Jane Bannister, now eight months pregnant. I ran into her recently at the grocery store, and we got into one of those conversations that only women can have just before closing time while frantically sifting through the dinner options. In the midst of giving serious consideration to a package of calf's liver, she looked straight at me and said, "I was in love with my first husband right up until the day I married Michael."

So I was about to be married again. But I did not believe that the man I was going to marry would be my husband. *You* were my husband, would always be my husband. And then there would be this other man, the man I'd live with.

Funny—it wasn't that long ago that I couldn't imagine living with anyone but you, couldn't imagine establishing that kind of intimacy all over again, reinventing another private vocabulary of silly names and gestures, exquisitely articulate only to us. And then marriage would mean that I'd have to be naked at times, unclothed in full view of another man, at the age of forty-seven, with my semicentennial soon to come screeching down the track like a runaway locomotive.

The real tug of history, I suspect, is the familiarity, the acceptance. You knew me when I didn't come up-holstered with broken capillaries and other assorted der-matological excesses. Tucked in some fond corner of your memory was the Original Woman, the unweath-ered me. But Edward—bless him!—actually fell in love with this decrepit pile, complete with all the attendant middle-aged features. But, of course, as my periodon-tist, how could he complain? It was the very fact of my deterioration that brought us together. What sweet thoughts he must have had as, week after week, he cut away at my gums while I lay back, bleeding into my paper bib, the tears gathering in the corners of my eyes.

"You can rinse now," he'd say more tenderly, I suspected, than was his custom. From the beginning it was a relationship based on trust. He would spare me the humiliation, the cost to my vanity, of losing my teeth; I would pay him regularly, in modest, for-writers-only installments. "My mouth," I told him finally, "is yours."

The operative word for the wedding was "under-stated." We were getting married, but we didn't want to draw too much attention to the fact. Who but somebody who's done this before would get married on the front lawn of a summer rental, wearing a beige dress?

Thanks to the drought, I blended right in with the grass. Anyone watching from more than fifteen feet away would have seen a string of pearls and a gold bracelet waving uncertainly through the air beside a man in a blue suit.

Early that morning, as I, the blushing bride, was

out gathering daisies, I couldn't help reflecting on how different this was from *our* wedding. I don't mean just the size of it, although it has been somewhat instructional, not to mention economical, to find that I am currently in touch with precisely four of the two hundred and fifty people present at our wedding, and that two of those are members of my immediate family. There is no safety in numbers when it comes to witnesses to wedding vows. Odd, though, that this time I was more nervous than I was in 1964. In 1964 I didn't have enough imagination to be nervous. I was someone, remember, who thought she was avant-garde because she wore a black turtleneck jersey.

Certainly things were simpler then. You packed up your mattress and your cinder-block bookshelves and you got married. Now there were two halves of two different property settlements, two conflicting universes, plus two sets of children, teenagers, no less, each operating with vastly different gene pools.

Not that anyone could easily accept, in addition to unplanned offspring, many of Edward's beloved possessions. Among them his bathrobe, a multicolored kaleidoscopic nightmare with a shawl collar trimmed in yellow braid. This to hang on the back of my bathroom door. But in the last year, as his partner-in-residence, I had already managed to absorb the overload. Was there a choice? Edward was a package deal. He came with all the standard equipment, plus extras. I could accept all or none.

But I wondered, now that the deed was done: Did

one send out stepmother announcements? Officially, I was an item in transition. Delivered: To writer Emily Moore, two teenagers, a boy and a girl, in Philadelphia, August 19, 1989.

The empty nest in which I had looked forward to spreading out was mighty full again, an object lesson in reality. Edward had stepped down off the screen, like Jeff Daniels in *The Purple Rose of Cairo*, and completed the metamorphosis from romantic hero to father, a man encumbered with a sixteen-year-old and an eighteen-year-old, plus the requisite number of high-fidelity sound systems, portable telephones, posters, and what every extended family needs, a larger-than-life cardboard cutout of Meg Ryan and Dennis Quaid as they appeared in *D.O.A.*

Was I equal to this task? Of course not. Next to actually being pregnant, this was the worst thing that could happen to a woman of my age and psychological limitations. I have frankly regarded it as punishment for my sins. Women didn't get away with it, did they? From the Bible to *The Good Mother*, a woman didn't venture outside her marriage, even to enter into another, without paying a price.

I thought of none of this at four o'clock that Saturday afternoon. What I thought of was you. I was happy, and I knew I was doing what was right for me. But in my perverse fashion I wanted you there because I wanted you to see that for yourself. After years of agony and uncertainty, I was finally shutting the door on us. I knew that you would never again be my friend, that the loss would be painful and permanent, that every day for the rest of my life your name would form itself at some unsuspecting moment at the back of my mind, and I would mourn the time when I had you to talk to.

As you can see, this is not the first time I've written to you since we separated in that dreadful 1984. There are roughly five years' worth of uncensored thoughts here. My intentions were to send them as I wrote them, but somehow I never did. I'm glad now that I hung on to them. This seems a better time; we've moved on. Besides which, all that is contained here belongs as much to you as to me.

Twenty-five years ago we started out on a wonderful adventure. It's still inconceivable, still excruciating, that the adventure has ended. But it has, and in the process much has happened to alter my view of you, of me, and of our life together.

You may think that much, or possibly even all, of what I say in these pages is inappropriate, or represents a wanton disregard of feelings, or may simply be of no interest. Please understand that I wasn't concerned with being appropriate or interesting. Nor did I want to hurt you. I wanted to tell you my side of things; I wanted you to know what it was like. Whatever these—call them notes on my life—mean now, they began as my refuge. They were the way I went on living.

1984

SEPTEMBER 3

Nina called bright and early this morning to see how I was bearing up on the first morning of my life as a separatee. I was trying to sound brave, but I found myself actually laughing into the telephone. "You won't believe this," I said. "Nick forgot his ties."

I told her how you'd come to pick up Annie for school in a navy blazer and black turtleneck, looking like a bruise, because you didn't have any ties in your apartment. You'd apparently had a rough night and didn't see the humor in it. But already it seemed to me that everything we did fell into this hilariously classical mode. Like my father calling my mother the night after he moved out to ask her if there was something wrong with an egg that didn't float when you dropped it into a saucepan of water.

Nina thought it was funny. Nina is going to keep me sane. Nina, Dr. Bloom, and Dickens.

SEPTEMBER 11

I got a letter from Peter this morning, the first he's written to me as a college student. I ripped it open with the same eagerness I had when he wrote from camp, and I had the same sickening feeling when I read it as I did then, crying at the kitchen table. It was almost as if he'd written those very words—"I want to come home. p.s. I men what I say in this leter"—though of course you can't say that when you're nineteen. You write down the data: How many hours in the registration line, how many courses you're taking, which ones. So the letter that devastates your mother is the letter you don't write. You don't write what it feels like to start down the road to college, leaving the people and the place that have been the core of your whole life just as it's all going up in flames behind you.

However much trouble he's having adjusting, I'm probably having more. It's hard to lose both the men in your life at the same time. I very much needed him to say that he thought he had chosen the right school, that he thought he'd be happy, but also that he missed me, that he missed home. But, for him, there's no *home* home. We've robbed him of that. He can't even be homesick. The very idea of home makes him sick, I'm sure of it. That Peter's a private person, sensitive and self-contained, makes it worse. Crying or shouting or kicking the furniture would have been facile, insubstantial for him, and would have trivialized his pain. I wish he hadn't appeared to take the news so well. It makes me nervous.

The men in my life don't say much, do they? We have a working relationship on the phone, you and I. Like Peter, we deal with the data. But there is the unspoken other life that runs concurrently beneath the surface. That's the real life, and the reason I write to you.

OCTOBER 4

It was probably the summer we were reading *Dinner at the Homesick Restaurant*. That's the way I remember time now, by what we were reading. Other people have a Proustian sense of smell that makes them remember, or they have a visual memory of, say, the way the light looks in different seasons. I have some of those associations. Honeysuckle will always remind me of June evenings when I was little and allowed to stay up late and play on the swing until my father came home. With me, though, it's mostly books. Books define the summer, and summer has been the barometer of our marriage, the time when anything menacing lurking in the background is apt to be felt.

I was thinking about this yesterday in Annie's room. If there were anything I wanted to forget about our life together, it would be a mistake to go in that room. It's all there, tacked to her walls: baby pictures of her and Peter; pictures of the two of them in the bathtub; of playing at the beach; of setting off for camp; ballet class; prom nights; family portraits in which Dickens usually occupies center stage, his paw casually flopped across one of the children's legs.

Annie has gone rummaging through the family archives, those dusty, curled snapshots we never got around to organizing, and has even come up with some surprising ones of us: you as an infant bundled up in a baby carriage with a large stuffed rabbit; me at about eight, tomboy and future mom, astride a wooden railing in full cowboy attire.

This was Annie's world, her mother and father, her big brother, her friends, and her dog. It was our world, too, a perfectly wonderful world. But sometime in the last couple of years, between *Dinner at the Homesick Restaurant* and *Heartburn*, something started going bad at the core. There are no photographs of that disparity, no hint of when it was that the imperceptible evolution first began, and one of us wound up wanting something different.

I couldn't leave Annie's room for the longest time. I was wallowing in the past, wondering: How did we get from there to here? How could we possibly have gone from that magical, snowy night in Boston when Peter was born to this day, and the next day, and the next, when you won't be coming home for dinner?

OCTOBER 13

With respect to the question everybody asks everybody but me—"Did he leave her, or did she leave him?"— I'm thinking of getting a bumper sticker. On the other hand, I might be putting myself at a disadvantage. "He left me" is the badge of the undesirable. No one wants a woman who's been dumped. But a man? The word is barely out before lines form with the thousands of women who want to kiss it all better.

You think I exaggerate, but I can quote you actual statistics. If one thinks of life as a game of musical chairs, there are roughly eight million women who don't have a place to sit down when the music stops.

Meantime, I've been to a party! (Having found myself suddenly in such social demand, I had to beg off on a second invitation, to attend a candida support group sponsored by the health-food store.)

So this was my first, albeit rather exclusive, party. I say "exclusive" because it was hosted by none other than Isabel Lyons, who is, as you know, another local rejectee, as were all of the other guests. A stellar group. Had I left you, I would never have been invited. So there was that one prerequisite, the perception being that we were all abandoned, emotionally devastated, sexually deprived, middle-aged women suffering from terminal loneliness who were desperate for something to do.

"The important thing," Isabel had said when she called, "is to keep busy."

As it happened, I had been quite busy, busy at not being any of those things. Frankly, I didn't want to be linked with the Victims. That wasn't the way I saw myself, as somebody to feel sorry for. They were all running out and buying *The Road Less Traveled*, whereas I got more out of Miss Manners's "Advice to the Rejectee." ". . . A broken heart is a miserably unpleasant thing," she writes, "making one feel ugly and unattractive, an enormous disadvantage when courting others."

That was the next step, wasn't it? Courting? One day, I might be ready. In the meantime, if I felt ugly and unattractive, it was only in your presence. When you said you were leaving, that was when my modesty returned. I was suddenly shy getting dressed. My body cast me in shame, as it had when I was thirteen and nothing seemed to be growing according to the normal plan. The horrors of the girls' locker room returned, and, once again, I became deft at sliding one garment out from under another. The nightgown was over my head before the shirt slipped off my shoulders.

There were the three months before you actually left, three months in which I never let my body out from under cover, never let you see all that had turned unlovable. I was still your wife. But I was diminished by being naked in a room with a man who no longer wanted me.

Now you insist on coming to pick Annie up every day. You walk in the house, play with Dickens, pick up your mail. You're all shaved, showered, and dressed for work, smelling like Gilette. I'm in the kitchen, cooking French toast, wearing a flannel bathrobe, my hair pressed to my skull as though I'd been sleeping in a sock. I look like a George Booth cartoon. Every morning I think, This man must be looking at me and saying to himself, "Boy, did I ever do the right thing."

What I want is a chance to be seen through new eyes, to regain my equilibrium and confidence. To see *myself* through new eyes. I like what Betsy said when her marriage broke up: "It's as if Ted was green and I was blue, and then we got all mixed up for twenty-six years. Now I want my blue back."

And there we have it, the real common denominator at Isabel's. We were all searching for our blue, that pure, undiluted strain of the people we used to be.

Picture it: Six women on the verge of estrogen drain, whose husbands had all departed for greener pastures, getting together for dinner on a Saturday night. The first thing I thought of when I walked in was that line of Lily Tomlin's: "We're all in this alone."

Isabel seemed a little nervous in the beginning, a hostess accustomed to functioning in concert with a host. She lit a fire—her first. She was admittedly shy about this, apologetic for having maintained such stereotypical roles throughout her marriage—during the Women's Movement, yet. Most of us were chopping wood just to make a point. But who was I to comment? I was already worried about Thanksgiving, when, in front of the children and my mother, I would have to carve the turkey.

Still, there was an air of conviviality at Isabel's, as if we'd gotten through the worst, and now each of us could sit back and appreciate the situation for what it was—a great story. A few bottles of Folonari, a touch of drama, and we were off.

I should preface this by saying that it had been an interesting few weeks. It seemed that everyone we knew whose first child had just gone off to college was getting separated. I'd be in the market, buying the "small family" loaf, when suddenly someone would seize my upper arm with a white-knuckled grip and say, "Get this. Reed comes home from the hardware store on Saturday and announces to Libby that he's leaving. He's in love with someone else. In twenty minutes he's gone. Can you imagine?"

No, I really couldn't imagine, and I know you couldn't, either. We were always incredulous hearing stuff like that. The first thing we'd both say was, wouldn't you *know*? How could you live with someone and not know a thing like that? Well, that's what most of these stories were like. And the timing. God, do men ever have a knack!

There was Rob. He didn't say a word to Claire until the weekend of their twentieth-anniversary party, with dozens of old friends about to descend on them from out of town. For weeks, Claire had been going over menus with the caterer, fixing up the garage apartment for the man who had been Rob's best man and his wife, potting new plants for the terrace, making sure everybody had a place to stay. The whole time, he'd been strangely removed, like a part-time employee waiting for instructions: "Where do you want this to go? What do you want to do with that?" She asked him a couple of times whether anything was wrong, but he said no, he was fine.

The Friday night before everybody was due to arrive, Claire was running a bath and sitting naked on the edge of the tub, cleaning potting soil out from under her fingernails. Rob came into the bathroom and began flossing his teeth. She was exhausted, and feeling a little wistful, so she asked him whether it wouldn't be nice if, after the party, they went away for a few days, just the two of them.

He didn't answer; he just tossed the floss into the toilet and went into the bedroom. Claire followed, staring at him, as if to say, "Well?" Finally, looking at her for the first time in months, he suddenly screwed up his face and started to cry. Then he told her about Charlotte, and Charlotte's six-year-old. He would be moving in with them, four blocks away.

Claire said she couldn't decide which was the

greater humiliation, that he was telling her the marriage was over and there was another woman, or that he was telling her the marriage was over and there was another woman while Claire was standing there without any clothes on. Listening to this, I couldn't help thinking about one other galling thing. It's the men who cry. Tears, a big show. *See how difficult this is for me, see what immense pain I am in. Feel sorry for me, because I no longer love you.*

Then there was Isabel herself, who was out for a walk with Paul and trying to find out when, or if, they were ever going on vacation. They were supposed to have left for the Berkshires every week for the last five weeks, and he kept postponing it. Turns out he had a girlfriend, a former babysitter of theirs, who was about to take her final exams for her BA, and Paul thought it would be too hard on her at this time—Isabel dragged that part out, "at this time," precisely in Paul's pinched-nostril, I'm-an-attorney way of speaking—for him to go off with his family. A postscript to this story was that it solved once and for all what Isabel calls "The Case of the Errant Undies," a spare little number in flesh-colored lace that Isabel had found last spring under the sofa in the den. She knew they weren't hers, but managed to convince herself that they belonged to one of the boys' girlfriends, and let it go at that.

I won't go into all the rest. But I wish you could have seen how ridiculous all you men looked in the retelling. There is another side to those stories, we know that; but no matter whose side you listen to, one thing is clear: Women are either monumentally stupid or deliberately, desperately, blind. If something is wrong, they simply won't see it. In this one way, I felt lucky. You and I were not like that. There was no other woman. There was no lie. What you said was sad, but I had to believe it. There just wasn't any other explanation. *We want different things. It's no one's fault.*

OCTOBER 15

I went with Nina and Stephen last night to see *The River* with Sissy Spacek and Mel Gibson. We seem to go to movies early these days. The theater was full of blue-rinse ladies and a few surviving men badly in need of nose-hair clippers. It's an awful movie, all rushing, angry water and screaming, hopeless voices drowning in the wind. I got sick of looking at Sissy Spacek standing on the river bank, the strands of her long, drenched hair stuck to her face, and those round, red, frightened eyes. My attention wandered, and I happened to see Stephen reach over and take Nina's hand. It was the first time since we've been apart that I've felt the sting, not of loneliness, but of being alone. I got this little ache in my throat, and wondered if I'd ever have someone to hold my hand again.

I've been so intent on not being the great walking wounded that moments like those take me by surprise. I try to be optimistic, to use this time to learn something about me and about us, rather than dwell on the failure. Sometimes I'm successful. At other times, a simple gesture, like a hand reaching out to take another, triggers all of my worst fears. For me, such a thing now seems so remote and improbable that I have to concentrate to remember the texture of your skin, the weight of your arms around my shoulders, the comfort of your presence.

I used to think of my mother, alone in her bed, the bed in which my father gave her back rubs on Sunday mornings, the bed in which they sat among their pillows and drank coffee and read the newspapers. How did she ever manage to absorb the loss of those small intimacies that comprise the larger, more encompassing aspects of love?

Nina has reminded me, in her usual glib fashion, that this is the best thing that's happened to me in twenty years. I don't like hearing that from a friend, *our* friend, supposedly. It seems mean, to say nothing of being awkward if we ever *did* get back together. Nina wants me to move on. It's as if she's taking my face and pressing it against the windowpane so that I can see beyond. What I see is an abstraction, an idea of something better for me. But that something doesn't take shape. I keep it at bay because it will have to wait.

I don't even know how to play this role yet. It *is* a role, the abandoned wife, just like being a wife is a role. You haven't played it before, so you have to play it as you've seen it played. I did what my mother did. I changed the sheets once a week, wore skirts-and-sweater sets, and used Minute Rice.

But here's where I stop copying my mother, and not just because of the Minute Rice. I want to interrupt the programming, make it turn out differently. As I said, I don't know how to play it yet. But while I'm figuring it out, I don't want to try anything fancy. I just want to be with my friends. Right now, there's nothing like Nina's voice on the other end of the telephone nearly every morning, checking in before she goes to work.

Of course, it's hard for me to believe that anyone who reviews restaurants for a living is actually working. Imagine going around worrying that you're getting behind in your eating. There must be days when she's bored and can't wait to hang up, but she goes on listening and listening. In some ways, it's merely the continuation of a conversation that's been going on ever since I met Nina. Love. Men. Women. Women and men. The limitations of men. Why men do what they do. Why women do what they do. What's wrong with what we do and with what they do. Dependency. Resentment. Guilt. Children. Hair. Dogs. Clothes. The bathing-suit problem. The body problem. Yeast. *Life.*

So this is our unexpurgated dialogue on the events as we perceive them. Nancy and I had another version of it when all the kids were little. They grew up around our conversations, literally evolved from one stage to another while we were talking. They outgrew their overalls, and then one day, when we were making tuna fish sandwiches and talking about the G-Spot, we noticed that their voices had changed.

To some extent, Esther and I had this same kind of dialogue until she moved, although Esther was always very guarded about her thoughts. She was emotionally stingy, more like a dealer than a friend when it came to feelings. I had to show her mine first, but maybe that was the only way she could afford to give anything of herself. But it's that giving-over of self that I find so specifically germane to women. I used to think that most time, I'm reminded of that passage in *Justine*, after she's left Alexandria and Darley is disconsolate. "Whenever his memory of her turned a familiar corner, she recreated herself. . . . Sometimes she appeared walking a few paces ahead of him . . . She would stop to adjust the strap of a sandal, and he would overtake her with beating heart—to find it was someone else."

There's much more to the passage than that, but the last line is the one that haunts: ". . . he carried the consciousness of her going heavily about with him—like a dead baby from which one could not bring oneself to part."

"I haven't left," you'll say. "I'm here." But to me, you're lost. I have no access.

OCTOBER 23

Yesterday, I decided it was time I acknowledged that I was no longer married, at least for the time being, and so I went to the bank to deposit my rings in the safe-deposit box. It was a small, very private burial service. I sat in this tiny room with a long, steel box and the rings I had worn for two decades, and cried as quietly as I could into the sleeve of my coat. Naturally, I thought about the night you presented me with the engagement ring, the fractional but perfect stone, and dropped it as you took it out of the box; I thought about the two of us scrambling frantically around looking for it on the restaurant floor. For weeks afterward, I wished I could write, eat, adjust my hair, do everything with my left hand so that the ring would show more; how I picked my clothes out each morning according to what would set it off best; how, at work, I practiced laying my hand casually across the top of my paper while trying out writing my new name; I watched my hand in the mirror while gesticulating in animated, imaginary conversation. I was consumed with the notion of change, that in just a few weeks I was going to go from being a girl who shared an apartment with other girls—girls who wore Villager shirtwaists and ate powdered doughnuts and canned mandarin oranges for breakfast—to being a married woman, somebody like my mother, who wore stockings and sensible shoes and sat in a wing-backed chair with her legs crossed reading the current Book-of-the-Month.

We had all the answers then; nobody else—our parents, most especially—knew anything. The odd thing is, I still think we were right. I did not marry the wrong person. That's what makes this so painful. I don't have any regrets. I can't even get angry.

In that little bank cubicle, I got lost in time. In effect, two decades had gone by since I had gone in. Finally I shut the box and opened the door. Remarkably, everything on the other side was much as I'd left it. A few bank officers working at their desks; two or three lines at the tellers', moving quietly along; the usual friendly chatter among the depositors. On my way out, I walked naked among them, without my rings. Drained. Despondent. Like any woman leaving a funeral.

OCTOBER 27

I hate to open with bad news, but here it is: The dish-washer has been operating exclusively on a forced hot-air system lately, spewing hard little granules of Cascade all over the dishes without benefit of water. I may be the only person to apply the sandblasting principle to her dishes. Generally, I wouldn't take small inconveniences personally. But add to this the demise of the vacuum cleaner, *our own* Eureka Princess, and I am distraught.

If you recall, the Princess hasn't been entirely well for some time. It's had electrical problems; it's had motor problems; it's had hardware problems. For the last six weeks it wouldn't close its lid, and it had to be carried around, like a great yawning baby, on my hip. But these have always been minor wrinkles in the Princess's otherwise long and happy life; like those in the marriage of its owners, they could always be ironed out.

Finally the Princess told me something: It had gasped its last breath. The suction had gone out of it. Somewhere, stuck in the length of the hose, was a mass. I'd shaken it, slammed it against the side of the house, but nothing came out. So this morning I took the last resort. I scrubbed up and performed a tracheotomy.

The operation itself, performed with an L. L. Bean knife, a clean incision of about eleven inches, was a success. I found the mass, not the usual Baggie twist-ties and dog hair, but wads of yellow tissues and cotton balls. Annie had cleaned her room. A helluva way to empty a wastepaper basket.

I sutured the wound firmly with tape, but something went wrong. The hose collapsed and flattened, like a tapeworm. When I plugged it in, the sound the Princess gave off was faint, unfamiliar, and heartbreaking. It came from the grave.

So there's been a death in the family, a metaphor for broken dreams. I feel, somehow, as if I've cracked the last dish of the good china. I look around my kitchen floor at the scattered remains of an era, and know that I'll have to reconcile myself to the fact that some things just can't be fixed.

In the meantime, I need help with at least some of these things, like the dishwasher. They are still ours. And if we wind up putting the house on the market, there have to be working appliances.

You say you're not going to pull the ball out from under me (whatever that means—who stands on a ball?). But as I understand it, you've agreed to pay the real estate taxes and utilities, even though you "don't have to do this." Getting out my slide rule, I find that that comes to a grand total of $3,000 a year. It doesn't seem that much of a hardship for a tenured professor/ painter—a whopping 4 percent. Well, Dickens and I put our heads together this morning and came to the conclusion that if we cut out all nonessentials, like car insurance and Milkbones, by February we'd be like Dustin Hoffman as Ratzo Rizzo, sick and hungry and poor, living in a filthy, cold room and dreaming of Florida.

Yes. You said I'd have to manage like "any other single woman." Fair enough. I just wish I'd had a touch of clairvoyance twenty years ago, when we talked about how important it was for mothers to work around their children. So much for "second incomes." So much for writing a column about family life for a women's magazine. instead I should be writing one called "Creative Financing Among the Disenfranchised." It's an honor to be a contributing editor of a major magazine, and it looks good on a résumé. But I'm still earning less than anyone I know, including the woman who comes to clean the house. I've always known that something was awry. She calls me "Emily" and I call her "Mrs. Washington." Having abandoned all pretense of solvency, I've had to cut her back to every other week. Even then, I felt more like her employee than her employer. "Don't you worry yourself now," she said, flashing me a big, brave smile. "You'll be doin' better before long." Stephen was telling me recently that it was bad enough when his first wife left him and the marriage was over; but when the friendship went, that was the worst thing.

I felt that she was in my corner, so to speak, the way I used to feel about you. That's the hardest part for me, knowing I've lost my cheering section. You were my friend, my partner. But you make it so hard for me to get back on my feet. What is it, Nick? Do you want me to fail, so that you'll feel justified in leaving? *Look at her; she can't even manage like any other single woman.*

Whenever I mention to Nina that I miss your friendship, she manages to let me know that what I thought was friendly didn't look so friendly, particularly in the last year or so. I keep writing that off; she didn't, *doesn't*, know you. Signs are clearer, though, when read from a distance. I knew you too well, or so I thought, to read carefully. I skipped some words, filled in the blanks with background information. I made assumptions.

I did feel, always, that you were on my team. That's been my image of you and I never questioned it. I never turned to find the person alongside me running in the other direction. Whatever it is that others seemed to have noticed, I missed.

You were supportive, affectionate, sensitive, and considerate—I can't have imagined all that. You were the man who burst into my apartment with flowers and cold remedies when I was sick. I blew my nose and listened, rapt, as you read from slim volumes of romantic musings by obscure poets. My roommates were jealous. I'd found someone I could talk to. You weren't self-absorbed or precious, like the men they'd met. You weren't even like the men they *liked*. You were a nurturer. And—the ultimate, as I heard it years later in women's support groups—you never left dirty underpants lying on the floor for somebody else to pick up. In so many ways, you were different. Far from being threatened by my accomplishments, you were proud of them. You took me seriously. You supported my work, you talked to me, encouraged me. How could I not have loved you, done anything for you? I got *so much* back. I'm incredulous now to see that when I wasn't paying attention, you became somebody else.

OCTOBER 31

Last year, on Halloween, I went as a dog. There are some, including you, who might have said I went as a dog every year, but never mind. On that occasion I took special pains. I had the benefit, too, of a model, our own real dog, who sat cooperatively and watched as I applied the corresponding markings to my face—a freckle here, a freckle there—until there were two identical black-and-white dogs, one 100 percent fur, the other 100 percent felt. Exclusive of ornamentation, that is.

"Ornamentation," if you recall, had included a thick, viscous layer of "Theatrical White," with which I had colored in my blaze and my muzzle, and an inky black that covered the rest of my face. Some liberties had to be taken, of course, with the mouth and nose, which given certain anatomical differences were difficult to duplicate. On close inspection, something distinctly undoglike could have been detected about the eyes. Otherwise, I was perfect.

Well, that was last year. This year, I'm not sure I want to go as a dog. It's not just as a matter of principle, that I wouldn't go as the same thing two years in a row. It's that this year, behind the scenes, something's changed. I'm no longer a married woman.

It was one thing, as a married woman, to paste my hair down under a black watch cap from whose sides dangled a pair of great, long floppy ears, and smear my face—including the insides of my nostrils—with clown goo. It's something else entirely, it seems to me, to do it as a single woman. I no longer have that firm and affectionate I-love-you-in-your-flannel-nightgown-and-kneesocks base of support. While last year I might have been perfect as a dog, this year I would be less than perfect as, say, a potential dancing partner.

Granted, costume parties are costume parties, and being pretty isn't the point. Nor, as you know, have I ever been one of those party poopers who comes as she is and pretends that she's just come from a business function. Still, if there's anything I've learned in my short time as a single woman, it's that there's such a thing as being too good a sport.

I remember, as perhaps you do, too, that Halloween night a few years ago when, long after most of the crowd had sifted in, the doorbell rang. I answered it to find a gruesome-looking little witch with blackened teeth, a long, bubbly nose, and a high, squeaky voice.

"Just a minute," I said sweetly, stooping to the child's level. "We just might have one more treat." And then I caught it: A familiar expression on the witch's countenance swept across my consciousness. This witch, I suddenly realized, was no child. She was none other than our friend June, married June, who was having an enormous amount of fun running around the neighborhood, fooling people like us.

June had done time, as it were, as a single woman, and while doing so never once, by her own admission, would she have gone to a party as a witch. Or if she had, she would have gone as a good witch, a lovely, radiant Witch-of-the-North–type, with false eyelashes and golden hair. At least she would have gone with all of her teeth showing and a less horrendous nose. Things had been difficult enough.

As you know perfectly well, I've always been impatient with this line of reasoning. But of course: I could afford to be impatient. I could afford to look at a single woman and say, "It's a costume party, for heaven's sake, not a beauty pageant." I could afford to see the folly of a single woman's missing a great movie because there was no one to see it with, or in storing up ten years' worth of vacation time because there was no man in her life.

Now, with every minute, I'm less impatient. Circumstances do have an impact. Whereas once I went comfortably to movies by myself and to parties by myself and took trips by myself, now I'll go to movies by myself and to parties by myself and take trips by myself . . . a bit uncomfortably. I'll do the same things with a different attitude, a different perspective. I've always felt independent. Now I'll have to live that way.

All the silly, crazy things that single women do, like shave their legs, even in winter—the sudden, cold reality is that I'm going to do them, too. I'll wash my hair on Saturday mornings before I go out and do errands. I'll pay more attention to fashion, more attention to me.

So this Halloween, whether I go as a dog, or a witch, or Ronald Reagan, the underlying truth is this: Any way I look at it, I'm going as an unmarried woman.

To My Ex-Husband

I did not go as an unmarried woman on Halloween. I went as you. June and Harvey didn't think it was funny when I showed up at their door in my Nick Moore suit. They were flatly unamused at what I regarded as a rather brilliant rendering of the man who had left me.

Annie screamed when I appeared in the doorway of her room, but recognized it nevertheless as something of a historic event, and promptly called up all of her friends. Dr. Bloom merely shrugged when I told him.

"There could be any number of reasons why you dressed up as your husband," he said. "I have no idea why."

It was a bizarre impulse, I admit. And yet logical, in its way. Maybe it was simply that you were gone and that I was bringing you back. And don't forget, it *was* Halloween. If what you want is a costume, estranged husbands are easier to put together than, say, an elephant. All I needed was a tweedy jacket, wire-rimmed glasses, which I fashioned out of a flimsy hanger, and a more masculine profile—that is to say, a bigger nose, easily accomplished with some putty.

I can't explain my motives any better than anyone else can. One day, maybe, they'll be clear. But I was riding on some kind of creative high. I wanted to have fun, and who's more fun than the Littles? But obviously, June and Harvey weren't in the mood. I was so disappointed. They and Nina have been my life-support system. Never mind that the Littles have problems of their own; marital strife is far from a foreign notion. But they put it aside and take you in. I show up at nine o'clock at night for a glass of wine and maybe a little cry, and first thing I know, Harvey will be at the stove, fixing me something soothing to eat. Food always does it for me; I'm just not the pale, wan type, with that exotic, underfed quality.

Now here was this frosty reception, as though I were selling burial plots. Perhaps they were just stunned. I *was* stunning. Without saying anything, June went for her Polaroid; she always has had a sense of occasion. I felt that to her mind this picture already had a caption: *The beginning of the breakdown.*

I'm not having any breakdown. Maybe there's no single reason I did what I did; or maybe that reason remains to be seen. Maybe I just wanted to know what it was like to be in your skin. Maybe I'd know the real reason you left. Nina keeps saying there just has to be more to it than what you've said.

I don't know how I can worry about something as trivial as a failed marriage when, for the second time, we've elected a retired actor president. Harvey says that the most depressing thing of all is that after a while people will get used to it. They'll say, "Oh, he's not that bad."

In the meantime, Harvey still can't get used to our being apart. It's beginning to dawn on me why he and June seemed so aloof on Halloween. We were so close, the four of us, that they're going through all the usual recriminations of the injured parties themselves. It's as if we had broken up with the Littles. You could say, after all, that couples who have gone to movies together and to parties together and have taken vacations together have been going steady. And now we've torn the foursome asunder. But because we're all civilized, we're still dating—one person at a time.

For the Littles, it's like burning the candle at both ends. They have to be equally loyal, equally supportive, equally caring and loving to both of us. They have to, in addition, be equally critical of the one who wronged on behalf of the one who has been wronged—which means that they'll get pretty adept at seeing both sides of an issue. They'll see that while I'm completely neurotic, you, on the other hand, are completely neurotic.

Ronald Reagan can be with us for only four more years. You and I and the Littles mght be doing this for the rest of our lives. And that's what *I* can't get used to.

N O V E M B E R   9

Such indignities women suffer! I'm getting all of my vital parts checked out while I'm still looked upon favorably, if loosely, by your insurance carrier as "Spouse." Unfortunately, one of the parts is a relic that must be inspected at close range and, as things have developed at my family practice, by a man young enough to be our son.

In principle, I generally don't speak to anyone under thirty; but a gynecologist that young, especially a male gynecologist, should by law not be permitted to examine anyone over thirty-five.

Am I sexually active, he wants to know. No eye

contact here. Or here: Do I still menstruate? He seems
surprised at my fierce, affirmative nod. "Yes," I snap,
"and these are real teeth, too."
"Well, in a woman of your age . . ." he says.
A woman of my age. What am I, a biological phe-
nomenon? I'm forty-two. I've forgotten more than he'll
ever know about women of my age.

Why, suddenly, does the world seem overrun with
callow youths smelling of Clearasil and looking suspi-
ciously like earnest students on a class trip? I don't see
how my mother can stand it. But when I complain—
not of young women doctors, who at least have the
appearance of being sympathetic and seem to know what
you're talking about, but of young men doctors, who
don't—she becomes impatient. She has no interest in
going to a woman doctor. There are entirely too many
women in her life, she says. At work. In her apartment
building. At the hospital where she volunteers. On
travel tours. So when young, handsome Doctor Brooks
gave her an internal recently, she didn't feel like I did.
She said, "It was almost a pleasure, really!"

This from my mother, a woman who doesn't acknowledge that bodily functions exist. Do we ever
know our mothers? A *pleasure*—how is such a thing
possible? Believe me, this doctor was no pleasure. He
was arrogant, unattractive, and short, with small abun-
dantly hairy hands.

Do I sound angry?

Annie tells me you don't like the color I painted the
kitchen. Too bad. You've lost your voting privileges.
Anyway, it's a clean exorcism job, my version of washing that man right out of my hair. It's not actually pink.

To My Ex-Husband

I prefer to call it "Dusty Nipple," and try not to dwell
too much on the implications.

NOVEMBER 14

Thanksgiving—again. I hate it, I hate it, I hate it! That
sums up the holiday spirit when you ask a woman who
is newly separated and whose youngest child is still living at home and wishes she weren't because "it's not
home anymore," and whose oldest child may or may
not come home from college, and if he does, may or
may not stay with her, and whose sister and brother-in-
law may or may not come, and if they do, may or may
not bring their own children, who want to see their
friends and who, in any case, no longer have anything
in common with the woman's children, and her mother
may or may not come to dinner because her house is
always freezing. But if her mother does come, the
woman wants her sister and brother-in-law to be there,
too; otherwise it's much too quiet. The air fills with the
sound of swallowing. She stares into her mother's eyes
from across the table and sees recrimination, the inevitable, "What did you do to make this happen? No one
could have been more devoted than Nick. You never
learn."

The trouble is, just when you get used to not operating as a family, you have to think about operating
as a family. Here are the possibilities: a) We can all get
together here for a midday dinner, you, my mother and
the kids and I. That's if you think your presence here in
this house can be explained. (No one knows whether

it's anticipated, and if it is, to what extent, or by whom.) Or, b) My mother and the kids and I can have a midday dinner here; then, Annie and Peter take two Fleet enemas each and go over to your apartment to have another Thanksgiving dinner with you. Or, c) Annie and Peter go to your place for Thanksgiving, period, and I and my mother, who doesn't care much about food anymore, can share a Cornish hen.

A brief postscript to Halloween: I mentioned to Dr. Bloom that I was still getting phone calls from people like your sister, who don't seem to have been told that we're separated. His eyes lit up. "That's why you dressed up as Nick! *He* wasn't talking. *You* were talking." The unconscious works in mysterious ways. Like the Lord.

DECEMBER 2

I hope you had a nice Thanksgiving. Forgive me if that sounds sarcastic. Any hint of insincerity isn't directed at you, but at the situation. How long does a newly separated man have to know he's free for Thanksgiving dinner before the phone rings? Six, maybe seven minutes? It must be the image a single man evokes, standing all by himself at the microwave, waiting for his Swanson's chicken pot pie. He'll eat it with one of the two forks he bought at Conran's recently, along with two plates and two glasses, an apron, some dishcloths, a couple of wooden spoons, a mixing bowl, some bath towels, and a set of sheets, decidedly masculine, with gray stripes. I can see the saleswoman, too, very solicitous, very *Oh, poor baby*, leading the bewildered fellow around the store, saying, "Now let's see," as if speaking to a small child, "you'll need one of these . . ."

I have an extra set of measuring spoons, by the way, or should I send them to your hostess?

I can't wait until the holidays are over and we can get on with the business of being separated. The trouble is, being separated is a condition of suspension. It could go either way. Until which way is decided, it feels like an occupation. *How are you? I'm separated.* I'm so busy being separated, there isn't room for living. I'd be happy just to have people stop telling me how wonderful I look. What they mean is wonderful, considering—as though I'd just had a gall bladder operation.

Nina and I were talking this morning about how you know it's the last time. You often don't know it's the last time for a lot of things. The last time you scare somebody to death with a rubber lizard. The last time you sneak a look at your Christmas presents before Christmas. The last time you make out in a parked car. The last time—am I putting too fine a point on this?— you make love to your husband.

Nina says that, with Alec, she knew it was the last time. "He said, 'Listen, honey, it's the last time.' " She laughed. Of course, she wasn't laughing at the time. She was twenty-seven, with two toddlers, and Alec was about to move in with Nicole.

I wonder if what I remember is what you remember. Do we remember different things, or do we remember things differently? Where was it that we last made love, Nick? Maybe you think it was outside, under the clothesline at the house we rented last summer. You remember the way the legs of your khakis tickled your back as you rocked back and forth.

It was not under the clothesline. It was in that funny bathtub on the first floor, the one that was made for midgets. You said, let's try it, and so I wrapped my legs around you and you slid under me. But then we started moving and making waves. Bigger and bigger they were getting, until the water began sloshing over the side of the tub. I started laughing. I couldn't stop. The more you moved, the more the water leapt out of the tub, and the harder I laughed. Tears ran down my cheeks. You got furious with me, and so it didn't work. You grabbed your towel and stormed out of the bathroom, and I thought, it *was* funny. We could have at least had that together.

DECEMBER 12

I need to talk to you about money. One reason is that the gas company sent me a maintenance contract for the heater. Do I want a maintenance contract? I know that one of your longstanding grievances with me is that I never paid any attention to these things. It strikes me we had a pretty good balance there; you never paid any attention to cleaning the house or what we were having for dinner or who needed to get picked up at the orthodontist. It's interesting, isn't it? That while I'm over here learning more than I want to know about maintenance contracts, you've probably figured out that if din-

ner isn't any good, there's only one person you can turn
to. Separations are great for that. If nothing else, they
teach us how to be whole.

Now, about Annie. I'm worried about her. We're
into our third day of stony silence. She's obviously
angry and upset, but all she'll say to me is, "I'm fine,
Mom." She also won't let me do "Mommy things,"
like smooth her hair back or fix her collar. She was
probably never fond of "Mommy things"—what adolescent is?—but she usually indulged me.

Somehow we could have handled this whole thing
better. One of the problems is that, for Annie and Peter,
there isn't the relief that comes of a sudden cease-fire, the
stunning quiet after the last plate crashes in the corner.

There was no fire. Our yelling and shouting turned
inward, slowly poisoning us, breaking us.

To begin, it was a bad idea to tell them at dinner.
We should have taken a lesson from the Maple family
in *Too Far To Go*, which I've recently reread. Remember
that scene when the eldest daughter comes home from
France at the end of her semester, and they have this
lobster and champagne dinner? The plan is to tell the
children later, one at a time, but it doesn't work out that
way because one of the sons notices that his father has
been silently crying all through dinner, and asks why.
The son gets drunk and shouts, "What do you care about
us? We're just little things you had." Then the boy stuffs
his sister's cigarettes in his mouth, along with the nap-
kins, and chews them all up. A wonderfully written
piece of fiction that felt so real, so awful, that I thought
I was reading about us.

I wonder if Peter felt like that boy. "You should

have told us you weren't getting along," he says. The father answers, "We do get along, that's the trouble, so it doesn't show even to us . . ." The line goes on to read: " 'That we do not love each other,' is the rest of the sentence, but he can't finish it."
It didn't show to us, either. Or at least until recently it didn't show to *me*. So Annie and Peter were completely unprepared for what to them is a tragedy.

I wonder how many parents who decide to end their marriage think that was the worst moment of their lives, when they told the children. You're familiar with those movies of traffic accidents that you have to go watch at the local high school when you get too many moving violations. There should be a movie of nothing more than scene after scene of parents telling children that they are going to be living apart. It should be a legal prerequisite for all those contemplating such a thing. I have to believe that nearly everybody would reconsider. They would see their worst fears played out in the faces of their children, and they would take that extra step, cross the bridge, look back, see what it actually is they are about to do, and be repelled. If someone had shown me a film of that night, projected it big as life on the dining-room wall, so that we could have seen ourselves sitting in the candlelight—Annie struggling to hold herself together and clenching her milk glass so tightly that I thought it would crush in her hand, and Peter eyeing each of us levelly, coolly, and with absolute disgust as he rose from the table and went to put his dishes away— I couldn't have let it happen.

To My Ex-Husband

DECEMBER 20

I've been looking at the kids' Christmas lists. Somehow, I am not interested in giving them "Patagonia anything" or "gloves" or "watch like the one I lost." What I'd like to see is "red bicycle" or "basketball hoop." Toys. Christmas makes me want my children back. There are these tall, slender, young adults walking around, yes; but where are my children? I want Christmas to be fun. I don't want home to be the place where nobody wants to come anymore. Somebody stop me, please, before I go and do something stupid and compensatory, like buy a puppy.

Am I feeling sorry for myself? You bet I am! Blame it on the season. Dickens is a wonderfully warm and cozy companion, especially on lazy Sunday mornings when I let him up onto the bed. But he won't roll over for a hug on Christmas morning and badger me for hints about his present. That was the real Christmas, wasn't it? That little slice of time to ourselves before the kids got us up, and we lay in the snowy blue darkness of early morning, giggling under the blankets and guessing. I loved the elaborate game we played just to put each other off when the guesses got too hot. Dickens is my Santa Claus now. I know he'll make a noble effort.

DECEMBER 26

How ironic to have had such a nice Christmas together just after separating. Not that it wasn't a little strange to have you arrive like a friend of the family, for the festivities, rather than as part of the pajama parade down the stairs. But that moment quickly passed, and it seemed almost as if you'd never left. Which is a problem: How to resume the separation.

My heart went out to Annie and Peter, how courageous and strong they were, making such valiant efforts on our behalf. It's dangerous, I think, to view your marriage as it's reflected in the eyes of your children. But I thought they were saying, in effect, "Come on, you two, take a second look, see how beautifully we fit together. Just love each other. Is it that hard?"

Their grown-up behavior made me feel childish and petty. What possible grievance could we have that compared with the family, with the well-being of our "team"? The day worked because of them—and the incomparable Nina. It was a risk. I doubt she even thought about it; she just has that go-ahead impulse. I can just see her riding down the escalator in Bloomingdale's and, suddenly, her eyes are like pinwheels. There they are, *carrot slippers*—perfect!

I had my problems preparing dinner while shuffling about in a pair of twenty-four-inch vegetables in brilliant orange, but I think we'd agree that the atmosphere they created was worth the extra effort it took to get within arm's reach of the stove. What was great was that the kids got as much of a kick out of them as we did. Our job has always been to make Christmas a happy time for them; this year, they did it for us.

Is that all we were doing, though? Rising to an occasion? I'm not so sure. It isn't that we don't love each other, it's that we ceased to make the effort. I keep having this feeling that we're sliding toward a divorce neither of us really wants. And I have to ask, are we letting this happen, or are we making it happen? The answer is, we are not making it not happen. When it's all over—is it only then that we'll ask, *Why? Why in God's name didn't we make the effort?*

1985

I shouldn't complain to you about my lack of privacy, but it occurs to me that scheduling a good, productive cry has its inherent difficulties, like having an affair. By the time you've seen your child off to the movies, put a spare key under the plant in case she comes back for something, left notes for all of her friends who might conceivably stop by, unplugged the telephone, and flung yourself dramatically across your bed, holding a box of tissues, you're not in the mood anymore.

I do know, of course, that this is the up side. I've lost my privacy, but I'm not lifted out of context. My life has changed, but I have all the familiar trappings: the furniture, the paintings on the walls, the water spots on the ceilings, Annie and Dickens to wonder where I am when I'm late. All this inextricably associated with who I am. Everything, if not normal, has the appearance of being normal. It's just that you're not here right now.

But *you*. You come home from work and walk into a dark, one-room apartment. No one says, "Hi, Dad," or jumps up to lick your face. No welcoming aromas to whet your appetite. What you see are the harsh reminders of transition: an unmade futon; a door that doubles as a dining table and a desk; your half of the double boiler; a spotless oven mitt in a kitchen so small that it necessitates deciding, before entering, which direction you want to face once inside. This, the black hole of the separated man. The bachelor pad, the room at the bottom.

J A N U A R Y   1 5

I've been out getting a preview of Life From Now On
from one of the women in my exercise class. She's been
seeing this doctor, a resident. He's about twelve years
younger than she is, a fact that bothers her not at all,
which is something of a mystery since he says he'd like
to have children someday. You'd think that would
pretty much rule him out as a serious candidate. They've
had at the most four dates, and already she's offended if
he shows up without his overnight bag. Sex so far hasn't
been good for her. "I just don't know where I stand
with this guy," she tells me.

If not, why not? I don't get it. Women are beginning to annoy me. Yes, a lot of men are noncommittal,
and behave badly, but aren't they getting the permission
to do it—from women? Why should men treat them
with any more respect than they treat themselves? In a
rare gesture of intimacy, my editor, whom I met with
recently, leaned across her desk, lowered her voice, and
said, "So much of it, though, is the guys. I mean, don't
you think—really?"

We had been talking about miserable relationships,
nearly all those she knew. And all had to do with women
who were hanging on too long for too little by their
fingertips. After a while it became hard to listen. I was
ready for them to let go, to drop into the abyss and be
done with it.

My editor wanted me to write a column about emotionally impotent men. But no, I didn't think it was the

guys. I thought a lot of it was the women. You read an awful lot about why men are jerks. Even *men* think that most other men are jerks. But no one wants to talk about why, because so much of the why can be laid at women's doorsteps. As long as women perceive that theirs is the greater need, men will get away with what they can. A woman may say, "This is unacceptable; you can't do this to me." But just let that phone ring, and she's right there, ready to give him his last, fifteenth chance. Men have gotten the message, all right. And that message is, "I don't have to do anything. I don't have to be a decent person. All I have to do is show up."

More and more, I feel like someone severely disconnected from the world, as if I've only just been released from a long confinement. This woman I spoke of, she's out there, part of that world, while I hide behind my typewriter. She tells me that if I want to have any social life at all, I'd better get used to the idea of sleeping with men on the first date, because "that's the deal." Maybe this is my New Year's resolution to myself: *Don't get too needy.*

JANUARY 20

You know that little song you used to sing every time you replaced a washer or rehung a window? "It's so nice to have a man around the house . . ." It's a catchy tune, but time is running out if I'm ever going to teach Annie that it need not be background music for *her* life. So I've planned some home-improvement projects, a sort of mini-forum on role modeling. The first session started early yesterday, at Conran's, where I bought a set of bookshelves to hang above the bed. I knew it would be an easy project to begin with, because the woman who sold me the shelves said it would be "no problem." I would not, she assured me, have to hire a structural engineer. My thought, you understand, was that Annie would see how masterfully her mother could perform this simple but terribly useful task, and thus the screwdriver, like her hair dryer, would become a normal and congenial part of her life.

That was my thought. Her thought, as I laid all the parts out on the bed, was to ask me why I didn't call someone who knew what he was doing. Trying to ignore "he" as the personal pronoun of choice, I picked up the diagram that came with the instructions in search of some important clues, such as where, in the drawing, the wall was in relation to the shelves—not as easy as it might seem for a verbal, as opposed to visual, person. Next, I set about trying to identify all the pieces. The two long, flat parts I recognized as the shelves. So far so good. Then there were some curved things that I figured were the brackets. After that things got a little fuzzy, but fortunately June showed up with the drill and the drill bits I'd asked to borrow. I thought, at first, that she had brought me some freshly baked rolls, appearing as she did, like Little Red Riding Hood, with a wicker basket and an inviting red-checkered napkin covering its contents. You'd have thought the tools were contraband and I was breaking out of prison, which in a way I was. Anyway, she had all the pertinent questions: Where were the studs; did I need the bits for plaster or wood or concrete?

I responded with an expression that said, "brain-dead," an embarrassment that Annie took as an opportunity to excuse herself in favor of watching "Kate and Allie," who may have been having similar problems of their own. So I didn't know where the studs were. I could pretend, and walk around hammering my fists on the wall. But I'm a trial-and-error person; so, drill in hand, I would proceed in a trial-and-error manner. The possible errors, as I considered them, were a) hitting an electrical wire and going up in flames; b) drilling eight perfectly gorgeous holes that, for some strange reason, didn't line up; c) plunging too far into the plaster, and thus into the medicine cabinet on the other side of the wall, thereby puncturing a pressurized can of hairstyling mousse. Far worse than any of these, to my mind, was calling someone who knew what "he" was doing, some Tom, Nick, or Harry. Having been married to Tom, Nick, or Harry, I would frankly rather have died.

No one went up in flames. But as June and I concurred, there is some latitude between a twelve-alarm fire and a reliably secure set of bookshelves, especially when one is trying to fall asleep beneath them. So the good news is that the shelves are up—technically. The less than good news is that they may not support more than the thinnest layer of dust. I hesitate to open the window at night lest they sway in the breeze. In which connection (and for future reference), the molly bolt may have worked its way into my mechanical consciousness. Annie remains skeptical. But, as I said to her, in an offhand if unoriginal fashion, Rome wasn't built in a day. And—thank you, Woody Allen—eighty-five percent of life is showing up.

To My Ex-Husband

A rare occurrence: A phone call, not for Annie, but for me. An unknown male voice. "Hello, Emily? My name is Sid Pomerantz. I'm a friend of Marilyn Beck. I'm single, and you're single, and this is one of those conversations."

I laughed. Cute, I thought. But practiced, rehearsed. I wasn't talking to an amateur tonight. Quickly, we got through the preliminaries. How long each of us had been single, number of children, their ages—the stats. I soon ran out of questions. There was nothing further to do, as far as I was concerned, but meet the man.

Sid, however, was just getting started. Did I play tennis? No, I couldn't say that I did. Did I ski? No. But, I added in a moment of playfulness, I had had a great deal of fun recently sliding down a steep, snowy hill on something that looked like the lid of a trash can.

Sid was not amused. This was not just "one of those conversations" at all; it was an interview. I was being screened for acceptability. And, not incidentally, I was failing. It was quickly established that I did not take winter vacations in Utah, did not sail in the Bahamas, did not work at developing my true fun potential at all, while he was positively killing himself having a good time. I myself began to wonder what Sid had been wondering all along: What *did* I do?

I was a woman who slid down a hill on the lid of a trash can. I did not even have a toboggan or a sled. But Sid was nothing if not patient. Perhaps, he must have decided, I could be educated. I could develop an adventurous, competitive edge. We made a date for the following Saturday night.

So there I was, back in circulation. I was going to have a date. Just the word sent an unpleasant sensation up my spine. It carried with it a long, anguishing history of major disenchantment—alternating with minor disenchantment—from which, now that I thought about it, I'd never actually recovered. I'd expected by this time, you understand, to be living a rather peaceful and civilized life, anticipating the simple comforts of prunes and Polident. Now I was in the thick of it again.

I suppose it wasn't an atypical experience for a woman in my position, preparing for a blind date. Still, it had been twenty-two years since I'd last had a blind date, twenty-two years since I'd literally closed the door of my Cambridge apartment on the expectant tongue of a drunken bore from Harvard Business School at three in the morning.

Yet, as I ran around the neighborhood last Saturday afternoon, borrowing jewelry from my friends and soliciting advice, the years fell away, and all the attendant horrors of blind dating returned.

Only my roommate had changed since the days I set my hair in brush rollers and marinated in Sardo. It occurred to me, in occasional fits of anguish, that Annie and I were living the same life. We ate the same dinner at the same time and received the same messages. That is, no messages. He who preferred to remain anonymous would call back. I found myself listening to lectures I once delivered on the callowness of not leaving one's name. These were the words I swallowed along with the rest of my dinner—while pondering the possibilities, and inquiring casually (for a mother can never be too cool) as to the particular nature of what's-his-name's voice. I hadn't even met what's-his-name yet, who turned out, of course, to be Sid, and already Annie was walking around saying, "Emily Pomerantz. Hmm. That's not a bad name."

There were obstacles to overcome, though, before Mr. Pomerantz and I could get married. As I approached the bewitching hour, I began to worry not only about my appearance, but about the appearance of the house. Try looking at your environment through someone else's eyes, and insecurity abounds. I wanted to create the impression not merely of looking like a certain kind of person, but of *being* a certain kind of person, all because I was given to understand that *he* was a certain kind of person. As I've pointed out, the odds were bad. There were supposedly eight other women competing for this man.

All of which meant that I had to do something at once about that huge crack in the wall above the mantle. To us, it had been a cozy level of disrepair that we had come to accept, even appreciate, in our house as well as in each other.

Suddenly I had to get rid of it. I didn't want to appear to be the sort of person who didn't take care of things any more than I wanted to appear to be the sort of person who didn't take care of her body, who let herself go. I moved the vase of irises from the center of the mantle to the end of the mantle, where the crack was. It gave the room a casual, unself-conscious, if disturbingly asymmetrical, look.

Then I noticed the books on the bookshelves. A couple of them were reference books that had little numbers on the bindings, books that I had never returned to my college library. Not wanting to appear sloppy or disorganized, I tossed them, along with the carpenter's level and the hammer that I'd neglected to put away weeks before, into the chest that I'd been using to store Christmas ornaments and blankets. The little secret was safe so long as he didn't open the chest.

Next, I took the Linda Ronstadt record off the turntable and replaced it with *The Marriage of Figaro*, figuring on the strength of instinct that he was less a popular-music fan than a classical-music fan. Then, in deference to our telephone interview, I left the children's tennis rackets plainly in view. (If he had little in common with me, he might at least, as a selling point, have something in common with them.) By the time the doorbell rang, everything that could possibly be offensive had been removed. An exception might have been made for Dickens. (I didn't know if he was an animal person.)

I answered the doorbell with an optimism borne of confidence. I had dressed simply but elegantly. My hair, having done nothing to betray me, bounced buoyantly like the locks in a shampoo ad. I looked as terrific as I was ever going to look, and Annie, fortunately, was not around to tell me that I could have doubled as the headmistress of a girls' boarding school. Sid would be pleased.

What I had neglected to consider in this whole process, despite the odds, was this: What would please *me*?

The man could not have been nicer, if overly proud of his car, a red BMW convertible, which purchase I

imagine was the result of a middle-aged testosterone
rush. At least it hugs the road at 75 mph, which is more
than I can say for my neck. I'm glad the top wasn't
down. I'd have looked like Shirley MacLaine in *Terms
of Endearment*, after her hair-raising ride with Jack Nich-
olson.

We had dinner in Chinatown, where I stunned him
with my voracious appetite, which he accepted gra-
ciously, even appreciatively, as "amazing." I have to
say, it's nice to go to dinner with someone whose first
words upon sitting down aren't, "How about splitting
an appetizer?"

Nevertheless, "Emily Pomerantz" is not to be. I
couldn't say why, exactly, but there's a sadness in his
face that I sense is bone-deep. We said good night awkwardly, with a handshake. As he drove off, I wondered
just what you say when you're certain, beyond any
doubt, that this will not go anywhere, ever; that your
feelings do not warrant a second date. What is the best
way to convey that?

Trust Harvey to come up with the answer. "You
say, 'I'm pregnant by my father, and we've decided to
keep the child.' "

FEBRUARY 14

Valentine's Day, a day of cinnamon hearts and lace, sweets and sweethearts. I peruse the personals, searching for something that speaks to me, something singularly appropriate, like this:

> Single male—with crow's feet, "passion handles," and rapidly receding hairline—who has been known to get winded flossing his teeth, seeks female counterpart. If you are a self-proclaimed "true centerfold," a "fiery brunette," a "Dolly Parton–type blonde," a "Vanna White lookalike" or a "warm, vital, vivacious vixen" with great legs who combines beauty and brains, or are, in any manner of speaking, a perfect "10," you have no business answering this ad.
>
> Respondents should be cuddly without being well-endowed and be able to claim at least a few wrinkles and gray hairs. Nice legs acceptable; varicosities and spider vines preferred, plus a healthy supply of cellulite. You should have a nice, warm smile, but periodic periodontal difficulties are acceptable. Anyone under doctor's orders to "keep moving" has an edge. The prescription can be used as a metaphor for life.

FEBRUARY 15

Nina showed up late yesterday afternoon, just as the sun was going down and taking my spirits with it. I opened the door with my customary enthusiasm, expecting to see a meter reader, and there she was, standing proudly, almost officially, like a messenger from Western Union in six inches of melting snow and smiling broadly as she extended her arm, presenting me with a gorgeous piece of heart-shaped mocha cake.

Nina. My valentine. Women and the art of friendship.

MARCH 4

Is it possible to have an illicit relationship with your husband? I ask because it is a bit bizarre, running into you at parties, and having these flirtatious little moments with you, hanging around in doorways, exchanging meaningful glances over the rims of our wine glasses. If I didn't know anything about you, I'd be intrigued. I'd go home and call Nina, tell her in weighted, breathy tones that I'd *met someone.*

In fact, that sort of sexy, fifty-something woman with the gray hair, the violinist who lives in your building, asked me whether I knew you. She seemed interested. I said you were my husband. "Ohh," she said, her eyes following you around the room as we spoke. "We're separated," I said.

Her head spun back in my direction. "Really?" She was fascinated, less by you than by the fact that we were friendly enough to be at the same party. She thought there was something rather exceptional, even admirable, about that. Maybe the word she was looking for was "civilized." No "Correspondent," no third party, just two nice people who like each other, even love each other, but want different things and so don't live together, but flirt—on a good day, when they're not feeling angry or hurt.

I said I *would* be intrigued. Except that I know what this is all about. We're off-limits to each other now, and interested because of that. Are we suddenly going to be like other couples, who fall into bed when the husband comes over on Saturday to fix the garage door? I don't know why we should be any different; I just know that I want to be. Forgive me, but I see it as so much masculine maneuvering. *I can still bed her,* that kind of thing. I have actually heard those words. Yes, it takes two to participate. Usually, one is vulnerable, the other horny.

MARCH 15

About my birthday. I was touched that you called to ask whether I'd had a nice time. It was truly one of those occasions that filled me with a sense of being lucky, and rich. I find my friends more reassuring than anything I can name, not because they say sweet and flattering things to me, but because they don't. They're absolutely straight—and generous and funny and kind. Harvey made me the most exquisite garland of wildflowers and grasses. All night, I wore my garland and drank champagne and felt like a vision from *A Midsummer Night's Dream*. I felt secure and safe and loved. It was hard to leave. The party was a reminder that, in spite of much evidence to the contrary, I am capable of doing something right. I have chosen these people to be my friends.

On the way home, my car loaded with the little treasures that only people who know you well would think of, I thought of you. I wanted you to have what I have, wished you had had the time, or taken the time, to cultivate more close friendships. I'm alone, but I'm not lonely. It seems to me that you are lonely, and that is the difference between the lives we are making for ourselves. It's a difference that hurts me. It's not what I want for you, and though it isn't for me to say, I don't think it's what you want for yourself, either. And yet the decisions you make set you apart, and alone. Years ago, Harvey told me people really do get what they want. A simple, truthful statement on the surface. I'm still trying to understand how it works.

p.s. The other night when I stopped by with some of your books, I noticed an envelope on your desk. The handwriting was unmistakable: You'd had a letter from Esther. I didn't bother to mention it at the time, but I'd been wondering about Esther. I sent her a book for Christmas, but never heard anything from her. Now I know why. She's your friend, I mean that's the way it seems to have divided up. I got Nina and Stephen and Harvey and June. You got Esther. That's nice, I thought. I can afford to let go of Esther. It isn't that I won't miss her; I will. I'd miss her just for the books.

She always found the greatest books, slightly bizarre, the characters on some kind of an edge, like *Housekeeping*. For some reason, I could never get into the last few that she has sent us, the Annie Dillard, for instance, or the Isak Dinesen. Ask her how she liked the Fay Weldon book I sent, *The Life and Loves of a She-Devil*.

APRIL 5

How long did you think it would be before Nancy would say something? A secret of that magnitude, and you confided in Nancy, a.k.a. Gossip Central, before you told me. The woman is a walking bumper sticker. All I had to do was mention that I'd noticed when I went to your apartment that you'd had a letter from Esther. "I think it's really nice that Nick is corresponding with Esther," was what I said.

Nancy leapt at the opening. *"Well,"* she said. "You'll have to ask Nick about Esther."

So I took her up on it. And now I know about Esther. But it was Nancy's moment in the sun, all right. She basked like a snake on a riverbank, her tongue flicking at the opportunity as though it were a fly.

As the messenger, Nancy's an easy target. Nancy, my former best friend, Nancy, who disguised her essential misery with her immense charm. She never forgave me for not being fat.

I shouldn't pick on Nancy. It's just that I don't even know where to begin. I suppose I should be sitting here trying to figure out why, trying to understand, to make sense. *Why has this happened? What did I do?*

Isn't that what women do? In the end, they blame themselves. Somewhere I read that—that women see themselves as the cause when things go wrong, whereas men blame something external, some other person, a malady, an ulterior motive, the weather.

But right now I'm not interested in any of that. It's after 4 A.M. I can't sleep, can't imagine sleeping ever again, and I don't care about blame, or if blame is even an appropriate issue. All I want to know is, what was it like with you and Esther? What did you do to her, what did she do to you? If you'd kissed Esther, if you'd held her close, that knowledge would be enough; but that you traveled inside her body, straight into forbidden territory, makes my stomach turn.

Some would say I'm punishing myself, trying to visualize all this. But I want to know, I really do. Does she like the same things I like? Is she anything like me? My husband leaves me after twenty years and doesn't, until many months later, tell me the whole truth, doesn't tell me he was in love with someone else, had been for two years, had a secret agenda. He isn't the man I know, he's some other man.

You can't imagine how disorienting this is. If I could have named a single quality of the man I married, the person who has been at the center of my life for two decades, that word would be "integrity." Even in the tiniest ways, you were someone who never compromised himself. You had that core of wholeness that could not be cracked or chipped. A truly solid man. You were capable of being boring, stubborn, compulsive, irritating, judgmental, oblivious, and, occasionally, of having bad breath. But a word like "dishonest" could not possibly have applied. That integrity was your draw. It was the thing that made me the most secure, the thing I could depend on. Some women compensate for their own insecurities by marrying money, someone warm and loving, perhaps, but prosperous absolutely.

I married you because I knew, with a certainty that I'd have bet my life on, that you could be trusted. I married you because you were not like me. I was whimsical and impulsive and given to waves of elation and despair. I might fly away and self-destruct. You would keep me grounded.

This feels like a rape; the betrayal is that profound. It really would have been so much better if you had died. I heard a woman express that very sentiment once at a dinner party. "It's always best when your first husband dies," she said, stabbing a smoked oyster with a toothpick. It was delivered as a simple statement of fact, and I accepted it with a single knowing bark of a laugh. Certainly I had wished as much for my mother's sake. When, more than ten years later, he did die, it was too late. So much of her had already been trampled to death.

Now I see why, among other things, I seemed "just fine," as everybody said. Nina told me that it was amazing, I was going through all this stuff, but that I looked better than ever. True, I'd managed to have good days, but there had been some bad ones, too. I was on a roller coaster that I learned to let take me whichever way it was going. And yet, beyond it all lay a challenge, an enticement that I couldn't identify, some sparkling pool of untested water collecting on the horizon, like a diamond in time. A day might come when I would grab it and run.

And now this pain, searing and endless. There's nothing else like it. I keep thinking, *It could be worse.* Peter or Annie could have died.

My reality has been turned upside down. How could I have been so out of it? The lecture tours, the stopovers in Denver. What about the times Esther visited us? How did you stand my presence—by praying that I would fall backward down the cellar stairs?

I picture you two tearing across the room, flying into each other's arms every time I went off to the bathroom or to turn the chicken. Ninety seconds here, two and a half minutes there. The image is almost comical. Scramble, scramble, kiss, kiss and then, quick! Here she comes!

How does the busiest man in America have time to leave his studio? Or did you walk out on your students? Why wasn't it some stringy-haired postgraduate groupie, or a model from a life drawing class, some faceless female I couldn't appreciate your interest in? It's a bit ironic, all those times we played the Who-would-you-marry-if-I-died? game. Somehow, there's very little satisfaction in knowing that I always had it exactly right.

Where did you go when she was here, whose apartment? A hotel? One of those tasteful places with gold faucets and a hundred-and-fifty percent occupancy? If you weren't the busiest man in America, you were the poorest. See how you've managed to overcome the two revolving reasons why we could never do anything. Emily, *please.* I have to work. Emily, *please.* We don't have any money. Isn't it amazing, the obstacles you can overcome, obstacles as insurmountable as time and money, when you're in love? When I'm not thinking about this, I'm thinking about how stupid I feel. Or maybe it's naiveté. Whatever it is, I seem to have raised it to an art form. I always was that way. Even as late as college, when other girls were saying things like, "He only wants her for one thing," I thought, what? What's the one thing? People tried to explain it to me, and I still didn't get it. "Why," I said, "would anyone want to do that with someone he didn't like?"

This morning I saw Dr. Bloom on what you could call an emergency basis. He just looked at me and, in that voice that's so soft, so smooth, it's as if he's swallowed 3-in-One oil, said, "Nick's behavior makes a lot more sense to me now."

I love that voice, am hypnotized by it. But without even realizing it, I've come to associate it with bombs falling. The smoother the voice, the more terrible the discovery. My body prepares; it knows. My chest heaves, moisture oozes through my skin. My hands fly up in front of my face to break the fall. *Please. I don't want to know.*

I recall that voice speaking to me last June, when I told him that you'd gone to bed one steamy night with your jockstrap on. It didn't matter that I wanted you to take it off. "You're going to sleep with *that* on?"

I got the same weary response that I always got when I wanted something. *Emily, I'm tired. Emily, I just want to go to sleep.*

Sleep, with these poor, pink little buttocks bound

in a veritable highway system of thick, sweaty gray elastic. "It has to be," I told Dr. Bloom, "one of the ugliest articles of clothing known to man."

He laughed. He's not above letting me have fun with a story. Then he looked at me solemnly and said, in his 3-in-One voice, "I think that something is bothering Nick."

I keep thinking about that night at Isabel's. I wish I'd known it at the time. I wish I'd known that of all those women, I had the best story of all.

A P R I L   9

Nina has spared me. She refrained from saying, "I told you so." What she said instead was, "On some level, I knew it all along." It was that "on some level" that I was grateful for. What I thought she meant, of course, was that she knew there had to be someone. She knew there had to be more to your leaving than just, "We want different things." But it was worse than that. She knew all along that it was Esther.

Funny how you lock something in your mind without knowing why, a single word spoken in a certain way, a mood, a facial expression. The shutter clicks, and there it is, forever. I remember it as vividly as if it were yesterday, a sweltering August weekend that Esther came for a visit. I'm not even sure what year it was, just that it was unbearably hot. She had just arrived, and was standing in the dining room. She had a book, something by Susan Sontag, and she was telling you about it—and it was clear that she was talking to you, as if I weren't even in the room. I remember the look, an unmistakable look, lovely and exclusionary. It was a look of love.

There was a shy, breathless air about Esther at that moment, no doubt because she had just arrived, and there you were, right in front of her, literally taking her breath away. I even remember the way she stood, her left knee bent, her foot lifting ever so slightly off the floor. She was tense, excited, her rotten little toes curling in her shoe.

"Some of this is very difficult," she said, opening the book and turning to the place she had in mind.

It's stunning, isn't it, that a moment could so etch itself in your head and yet not register? But this is what I've been doing, all day, every day, highlighting the moments. They're not what I thought at the time, those moments. They're not what I thought, because while I was with you, every single day of the last two years, doing things that couples do, eating sandwiches and talking about remodeling the kitchen and cutting the grass and watching the kids orchestrate their social lives on Call Waiting, you were in love with Esther. It all looks different now, cast in a new and ugly light. I thought we'd had some good times, even in those last stressful months, and that nobody could take them away from me. But you managed to do it. You took all those memories—damn you!—and turned them into something I can never think of again without thinking of Esther. It's like looking at a photograph, of your son's graduation from high school, say, and seeing this shadowy figure lurking in the background. And you hold it

a little closer, and you think, My God! There's Esther.
There's my husband's lover. What the hell is she doing
there?

A P R I L   1 3

"How can you blame someone for falling in love?" This
is Nina's feeling, anyway. It's not exactly the cozy, com-
miserative comment I needed, but she's always felt that
way, even when she found out about Alec and Nicole.
Everybody said, "Don't you just *hate* Nicole?" No, she
really didn't. She didn't hate anybody. She just wanted
to die.

Well, I don't hate Esther, either, nor is Nina going
to do me the favor of hating her for me. But I can't be
Esther's friend. She did make a choice between you and
me. The fact that Esther eventually worked things out
with her husband doesn't change that.

There was one thing Nina said that made me feel
better. "What I can't understand," she said, "is anybody's having a choice between you and Nick and
choosing Nick."

I don't get it. I thought I was Esther's friend. But
friendship pales, apparently, in the presence of a man.
That's the great female malaise that makes a woman
rush, headlong, every time, toward the man, the generic
Man. Never mind that he's taken, or that he happens to
be married to a friend, or that she herself happens to be
married, or whether he's inappropriate in a hundred
other ways.

In time, I may soften my line on Esther, as Nina

has done with Nicole. Of course, it helps that Alec has now moved on to someone else, just as it helps me to know that it's over with Esther, that it has been over. But it is fresh for me, as if you had been in bed with Esther yesterday and still loved her today. I have to remind myself that it's been nine whole months since Esther left you in an August thunderstorm and flew home to tell Don what was going on. Their marriage may be better for it. I may even be generous enough someday to say I hope so. It would be good for the supermarket tabloids, too: HOW HAVING AN AFFAIR WITH MY FRIEND'S HUSBAND SAVED MY MARRIAGE!

I read something in a Miss Manners column once on the subject of faithless husbands. She said it was an old and ugly trick of society to pit the women against one another and forgive the men. She's right. It *is* an old and ugly trick, and I shouldn't bother playing it on Esther who, after all, may not be worth my wrath. She isn't the woman I thought she was. Nor you the man. Not because of the affair, but because of all the disguised weaknesses that were revealed. Telling me, for instance, as if I could be sympathetic, even so long after the fact, "Emily, I had two separations to go through." If you had been watching a play, you'd have loathed the character. You'd have said, "That worm." If being single has taught me anything, it's that nothing, *nothing,* is what it seems.

T o   M y   E x - H u s b a n d

M A Y 5

Ah, yes. To sleep. To sleep, perchance to dream. I know
there was a time when I went to bed at night and slept
until morning. I can't really imagine that now, can't feel
in my bones what it must be like. I'm beginning to look
deranged, nervous and big-eyed, like a lemur. It dawns
on me, finally, the full meaning of an acquired character-
istic. Because, in point of fact, I am getting awfully good
at seeing in the dark. By summer, I will have completed
my metamorphosis into a nocturnal animal and you will
be able to tell people, with some accuracy, that you were
once married to a small monkey. Do I sound insane? I
NEED TO SLEEP.

And yet I don't feel in the least tired. On the contrary, I'm oddly energized, racing toward my middle-
of-the-night high, when I write letters, or roll around
in my/your old bed and think delicious, murderous
thoughts. Years ago, I remember, someone in our
neighborhood created a scandal by suddenly leaving his
wife and running off to Florida with their babysitter.
The next day, that short, funny woman with the frosted
hair and the foul mouth who lived down the street came
over and said, "Honey, if that ever happened to me, it
would be on the front page." God, she made me laugh.

But the thing was, the reason I laughed was that I
knew it was true. It *would* have been on the front page.
One didn't mess with that woman. She was all heart
underneath, but she meant business.

Well, I wish I were more like her. I wish I were

a front-page kind of woman. Even my "murderous" thoughts are mild, as if I could be jailed for dreaming. Fantasies can be pretty dull if you don't know what you want. Do I want Esther dead, so that practically everybody I know can sit around and mourn? Death elevates. Imagine. My adversary, an angel. Angel Esther.

No, I don't want Esther dead. I merely want her miserable, in excruciating emotional pain, as I am. Death does not inflict pain in oneself, only in those one loves. So what are my dream options here? To take out a contract on Esther's husband—and leave Esther, the young widow, free? Never!

Would that I could appear like a devilish Puck beside Esther's marital bed and anoint Don with special, potent anti-love potion so that he would fall instantly out of love with his wife upon waking. Would that I could will abandonment into Esther's life, snatch away her confidence, her sexual juiciness, and leave her dry, parched, and utterly repellent. I want her all scratchy and prickly inside, like a stinging nettle.

But then Esther was never exactly cozy. Besides which, as June said when I showed her Esther's picture, "She's no beauty." But beauty was never the point, was it? You once told me that passion breeds passion. And Esther wanted you.

I need to know: Was Esther earthy? Was she raw with desire, in a way that I have never been? Was she the kind of woman, for instance, who never worried about whether she was going to leak little glutinous pools of sperm onto the bedspread, or, if you were being particularly intimate, thought back to how many hours it had been since she'd had a shower? I could never be jealous of who Esther is, but I could be jealous of her abandon. That letting go, literally giving yourself over, is the secret to so many things that seem just beyond my grasp.

JUNE 3

It's wonderful living in the dark. You should try it. Sometime, somewhere, when you least expect it, a light goes on, and you're pulled out of the tunnel. Let me tell you about my latest "light."

I am not by nature a suspicious person—as has already been established. But when Annie starts making a habit of cutting her telephone conversations short as I enter the room, starts humming, or launches into what I know instinctively is a change of subject, I take it that there is something that I am not supposed to know. Okay. Parents are not supposed to know. They may have what the military calls the Need to Know, but when it comes to their children, need doesn't enter into it. Now if she's talking about sex, or boyfriends, or about what a flake her mother is, that's not my business. But when I combine this with Annie's moods lately (part-CIA agent, part-ocelot), I have to think that this is not your typical adolescent frame of mind, at least not Annie's frame of mind.

So I began pressing. And pressing. And what do you know? The monosyllabic wall of stony impenetrability came tumbling down.

At that moment, she happened to be eating an after-school snack of peanut butter and Carr's crackers. Her face got all red, her mouth opened and, almost noiselessly, she started to cry. Peanut-buttery strings of saliva stretched between her lips as I pulled her close to me and buried my face in her hair.

"It's all over school," she sobbed, "about Daddy and Isabel."

Isabel? And here I was, still preoccupied with Esther. Not that there's anything wrong with Isabel; I *like* Isabel. She has a quiet dignity that has served her extremely well in these circumstances. But, for Annie's sake, couldn't you have chosen somebody she doesn't see every day, somebody all of her friends don't see every day, somebody other than the *school librarian?*

At first, I thought Annie had to be wrong. You and Isabel were just friends, I said. But as the words were leaving my mouth, I heard the doubt in my voice; I was the one who was wrong. And, of course, there was no doubt at all in Annie's mind.

She came out with an *Oh, Mom* I hadn't heard before. It wasn't that whiny, teenagey, "Oh, Mo-om, you-can't-be-serious, a *cur-few*?!" we've been hearing. It was grown-up and sympathetic—and yet impatient. It was "Poor Mom, you just don't want to see it, do you?" Anyway, it had the ring of truth. I couldn't have convinced her otherwise, so I didn't try.

Obviously, you can do as you like. We're separated. But I wish you'd at least have had the decency to wait until school was out. What a way for Annie to finish her senior year. It just isn't fair, when I think of what she's had to contend with already. She's done well, and should feel good about herself. Instead, she's crying and eating peanut butter and crackers and is too embarrassed to go to school.

When, Nick, would you have told me about any of this? Ever? It dawns on me with horror that if Nancy hadn't said something about Esther, I still wouldn't know.

When am I going to stop bumping into information as though I were living in a blackout? Is there more?

I feel as though I'm this dinosaur, dragging my way through a crowded village, and people keep stepping on my tail. "Watch out!" they're trying to say. But the message is traveling too slowly to my brain. By the time it gets there, the damage is done. I can't stop it. All I can do is stand there and let it hit me in the face.

The fact that you've chosen Isabel is not without its amusing aspects. She reminds me of the woman who used to do the Underwood deviled ham commercial, the tall, skinny, bookish woman with the huge black glasses who makes a move on the new tenant across the hall with her deviled-ham sandwich. She used to turn you on, maybe because of that dichotomy between the book and the bed, between the learned and the sexy, entities seemingly at odds. Dorothy Parker was wrong. It isn't true that "Men seldom make passes/ At girls who wear glasses." Glasses are like any barrier, such fun to remove. You want to claw your way to the real stuff underneath.

But the Underwood lady was years ago. *Years* ago. It's strange to think that may have been the genesis of your discontent, that our marriage disintegrated because of a deviled ham commercial, the woman you've wanted all this time, but never knew. I love thinking of Esther, my husband's now former lover, Esther the historian, who's even more bookish to my mind than Isabel, as a surrogate. And Isabel herself, the lady with hair the color of dust, and skin the pallor of an index card. I can see her sitting at her desk by the window, the June breeze wafting through the main floor of the library, luffing the long strands of fallen hair at the nape of her neck as she checks a stack of books in, flipping the covers— open, close; open, close; sliding the cards into their tight little envelopes. Is Isabel herself a tight little envelope? Is she thinking about you? Is our daughter sitting on the far side of the room, and scrutinizing her miserably over the top of her Greek civilization book?

Well, okay. *Okay.* So you're not coming back. You're not even thinking of coming back. And you were the Man Who Would Be Monk. Self-contained, isolated, abstract, the thinker. I never thought you were really that interested in sex. Not that you didn't like it now and then, only that there was no sense of urgency; there was no need. But there *was* a need, as it turns out. There just wasn't any need for me.

JUNE 21

Nina never leaves any room for doubt. "Nick's gone," she said. It was ten in the morning, and I was eating a Milky Way. Things usually feel a little bit better if I'm eating chocolate, but this was harsh.

"He and Isabel are probably doing all this great stuff." *All this great stuff,* I thought wistfully. I tried to wrap my mind around the expansiveness of the remark.

I had been childish, limited, ordinary in my lovemaking. I had held you back, and now I was paying for it with my imagination. You had replaced me in your sexual life, and there seemed no limit to what, with so little effort, I could put in the space I had vacated.

But I knew what Nina meant. It was time to close the door that I've kept open. That's what they always tell you to do: *Keep the door open.*

I didn't really need her to tell me that, or Dr. Bloom, who's been waiting for me to get angry. Whenever I wax sentimental, he shifts impatiently in his chair, crossing one leg, not just over the knee, but high up, over the other, as if he needs to go to the bathroom, as if he literally cannot contain his eagerness to have me understand. I know that I pay him to be on my side, to be *for* me. I've given him the information, the data, and I have to say, it doesn't look good for you. On the basis of the facts alone, you look like something of a creep. However, there are times when I think that if he really knew you, the way my mother did, or the way Harvey does, or anyone who saw for himself the delight we took in each other, he'd understand my sadness, my reluctance to let go. I just can't believe we're actually doing this.

"It is sad," he told me once. "But there were lots of sad things about your marriage."

Yes, I should be angry, am angry. But it doesn't last long. None of my moods lasts long. When I first started seeing Dr. Bloom, I told him I didn't think I was a candidate for suicide. When he asked me why, I said, "Because I have the attention span of a one-year-old. I can't even sustain my own depression."

J U L Y 3

Did you see me on Wednesday night? I saw you, turning the corner on three wheels. A *Wednesday* night. The holiday weekend hadn't even started yet, and you were rushing off, all spruced up, the after-shave probably still drying on your neck. I, anticipating my own glamorous evening, was on my way home from the 7-Eleven with a box of laundry detergent.

It was such a quick glance, a split-second caught in the shutter of the mind's eye. Your car coming toward me, fast; you at the steering wheel, hair slicked back, and then, as I rounded the corner, all was darkness in the rearview mirror. I thought, later, of you and Isabel sitting outside in her backyard, that delicious, summery scent of honeysuckle hanging in the air. It's barely even started yet, and already I want summer to be over. Everything's so fragrant and fertile, swollen with moisture. I feel my own barren hollowness. It's as if every move I make has an echo.

I suppose I'm jealous. But I don't want you. I don't want someone who doesn't want me. And yet, I suppose I should thank you for the inspiration. That sight, swift as it was, of you speeding through the night was a gun to my head. Move on, it said. Or prepare to lie down and die.

J U L Y 7

Jesus Christ. Something is awry in a world in which middle-aged women find themselves living in college dormitories over the summer. Peter's been at home for nearly eight weeks now, and it seems like eight months. When he first left for college last August, I was beside myself. We all were. Annie retreated to her room; Dickens sat under the kitchen table for three days with his bone and his ball and his frog all gathered around him. Poor dog. All the men in the family had taken off and left him to this little household of handmaidens.

One morning early that fall, I was out in the garden when old Mr. Williams wandered over. He said he hadn't seen "that nice boy of yours" for a while; hadn't seen "the mister," either.

"Peter's gone to college, Mr. Williams," I said. "And my husband no longer lives here, he has an apartment. Next year," I added matter-of-factly, "Annie will be gone, too, and I'll be alone."

He was quiet for a moment, taking it all in. Then he said, "Well, you got y'own self." I don't think Mr. Williams ever learned to read. But he turns out to be one of the wisest men I've ever met.

I was trying very hard then to get used to Peter's not being here, to get used to being a mother with only one child to take care of, to get used to not buying several pounds of cold cuts each time I went to the market, to get used to the verbal void, the sudden absence of those wry, soft-spoken comments that flowed effortlessly from his mouth. I missed him, missed not being able to find my *Newsweeks*, missed running out of orange juice, missed the tall, occasionally surly presence that never ceased to amaze me was my son. I wanted him near me. Having Peter here made life seem more normal. But somehow, I went from getting used to it to getting into it.

Dickens, meanwhile, is thrilled. We have some of our testosterone back. Tennis balls bounce off the walls, rugs fly, deep, manly voices fill the house—usually starting at eleven o'clock, just as I'm dozing off to sleep. Suddenly, it's all noise and boys, deafening, rhythmless music, and "Whaddya want to do, guys," and "Who's hungry," and "Mom, can I borrow your car?" Where is it written that the "Custodial Parent" has to double as a Siamese twin? Couldn't you take him once in a while, say, for the night shift? Or would that cut too deeply into your social life?

J U L Y 3 0

"You'd better stay married, because there's nothing out here." This is the advice, offered roughly thirteen years ago to Abby Berlin when she was debating whether to leave Bernie. I'm surprised I remember Abby's telling me this, because a separation in the early seventies could not have been further from our minds. Peter was learning how to read; Annie had just started kindergarten. How could anything have been more compelling than the launching of these two small, fragile people stepping out into the world in their Osh Kosh B'Gosh overalls?

Dickens was a mere fuzzy black dot in God's distant eye, but I have to think he was part of a grand plan.

So those words—*Stay married; there isn't anything out here*—did not apply. Today, on the other hand, they are a constant clanging in my ears, a bell buoy in a storm. With each successive wave, the truth crashes over me like an angry sea. Sid Pomerantz seems more divine every day.

"Up and down" is what a woman in my position says when you ask her how she is. I expected that. I expected to have trouble keeping up with my moods. What I wasn't so prepared for was the essentially solid plane of the day-to-day, like the Future that yawns before you after someone has died and the people who came to mourn have gone home.

In painting a bleak landscape, I should say that it is at least punctuated with some interesting, if infrequent, experiences. I'm not sure "interesting" quite describes the despair I feel for the woman—and I am one—who has the misfortune to believe, against a considerable body of evidence, that a man in one's life, while not essential, is a nice addition.

So in walks Walter Abbott, a slightly truncated version of Prince Charles, eminently presentable, eminently polite, eminently genteel—on first inspection. I, by contrast, was recovering from a summer cold, and was feeling unsavory in every respect. But he had tickets to the orchestra, and the program included two Vivaldi concertos that, as you know, would be hard for me to pass up—to say nothing of dinner at Dilullo Centro. A truly elegant evening, but for the fact that my nose looked as if I'd been washing dishes with it.

So we're having a brandy after the concert, and it comes to him, as he looks deeply, significantly, into my eyes, that there's an important phone call that he must make, and he must make it from his apartment. It seems the phone number and some of the information he needs are there. Reluctantly, I leave the restaurant with him, thinking, well, I can wait in the car.

I don't know what I expected from a criminal defense lawyer, but Walter has a tidily prepared case as to why it would be utter nonsense for me to wait in the car. My obvious caution offends him. Suddenly, I'm a six-year-old, a small moron, regurgitating my mother's advice, *Don't take rides from strangers, don't open the door to a meter reader without looking at his I.D.* . . .

All right. So I go up into the apartment with him, where I stand nervously in the foyer, taking in the environment, my eyes flashing from side to side like a cornered mouse. Walter's apartment reflects his personal appearance, clean almost to the point of being sterile, studied, and without warmth. Two quite lovely Vermeer prints hang on the wall above the couch; on the coffee table is a stack of Smithsonian magazines placed in an ordered, self-conscious way; the dining area contains a couple of dark, heavy, ancestral pieces that Walter's ex-wife might reasonably have considered adequate settlement just to be rid of.

Walter, meanwhile, has glided smoothly off across a polished parquet floor, as if on roller skates, to the telephone.

In a couple of minutes, he returns to find me perched on the edge of his chilly leather couch. He comes over and lifts me by the elbows, and then, pressing his hand into the small of my back, pulls me to him and plants a small, tender, premeditated kiss on my lips. In all honesty, I did not mind.

But a kiss, as the song says, is just a kiss. At least to me. To Walter, it was a permission slip. Suddenly the blouse is getting pulled out of my skirt, the buttons are coming undone. I'm busy retucking and rebuttoning. It's always the same tired scenario that turns what could be a really nice evening into a tawdry episode that leaves a bad taste in your mouth. Walter had bought me a concert and a dinner. And now, turning nasty like someone who'd been cheated, he wanted to be paid back. In retrospect, every sentence spoken, every gesture, smile, and laugh, all that I thought might develop into an easy affinity, was just an item in the final tab.

Ever the gentleman, he was willing to take me home, shoving me into my coat while telling me that I was a baby, that I'd led him on, that I was stupid and naive. What had I thought, anyway, that he just wanted my *company*? But I didn't want to give him that. I wanted instead to deprive him of doing the honorable thing. I stepped out onto 18th Street and walked over to Walnut, where I got a cab. Maybe I was a baby, I didn't know. I just wanted to go home and get in bed. Maybe next time I would remember something else my mother had said, rather recently: "Be sure to pay your own way."

A U G U S T 1 4

Dr. Bloom has a spot on his carpet. Yes, I know. I've
got to be the only woman ever to write to her estranged
husband to say that there is a stain on her psychiatrist's
office floor. But hear me out.

It's not an ink-blot sort of stain, the kind that looks
like either a bat or a boned chicken breast. I don't inter-
pret it. I just stare at it when I say certain things that
can't be said face-to-face, like, "I don't see myself mas-
turbating my way through middle age."

This was yesterday morning. I had been talking and
staring at this thing that I had silently focused on for
more than a year when I glanced sharply up at Dr.
Bloom, and said, "Aren't you ever going to take care of
that stain?"

He smiled and said—and this is what I love about
him, that he would just answer the question, straight,
as though I were a perfectly normal person—he didn't
know what it was, that it wouldn't come out. But it
occurred to me, now that I mentioned it, that there were
other things in his office that could use some attention,
like a vase of pussy willows that were turning to a pile
of brown powder. To make a rather minor point, a baby
step, as it were, I was moving away from my stain, my
beloved home base, and onto other things. I had talked
about masturbation and rejected it as a permanent life-
style, though other women I knew had managed,
through creativity, to find it satisfactory. (A friend once
told me she used her left hand because it was a little

clumsy and therefore terribly exciting, as if she were with someone new.)

But I was saying, whether I knew it at that moment or not, that I was ready to move on. And then I told him about my weekend.

On Saturday night, I had one of those trite, it's-a-small-world experiences. I was at a housewarming party given by a woman I met, years ago, at a women's support group. She's single now, as has often been the destiny of women who attend support groups. I had gone to see an early showing of *The Killing Fields*, which should tell you what kind of mood I was in. I was in the mood for lying on my bed and slipping quietly into a coma. I thought, though, that if I forced myself to go, there was a good chance I'd develop a better frame of mind in spite of myself. I also had to obey my own rule of thumb, which is that the party you least want to go to is the one you should go to. Maybe it's just a matter of having negative expectations; but somehow, those are the ones I'm glad I went to. And who, I ask you, would expect to have a great time at a party for which the hostess has hired a magician?

For the first hour, we sat through the forced applause of people who are all wondering the same thing, on the order of, What do I have to do to get out of this class? Between tricks, I'd cast an eye around the room, looking for an unobtrusive way to get to the bar. Finally, I escaped upstairs to the bathroom and found this man sitting in the hallway, reading a book. It was a thin book—but still, not a good sign if you're a hostess.

But the bathroom was occupied, so I sat down next to him, and glanced at the cover of the little volume,

which turned out to be *Small Pig*, a diversion he'd grate-
fully found on the stairs. I told him it had been one of
my daughter's favorites. "Really?" he said, and started
to read.

". . . But most of all, Small Pig likes to sit down
and sink down in good, soft mud." He was getting to
the part where the farmer's wife goes on an out-of-
control cleaning spree and cleans the house, and then the
barnyard, and the stable, and the chicken coop, and the
pigpen, until poor Small Pig has no mud to sink down
in. I started to laugh.

"You like this part," he said, turning to me, smiling. I always did like that part, the ultimate case against
vacuum cleaners. Now what made me laugh was the
idea of these two grown-ups, who didn't even know
each other's names, sitting on the floor and reading a
children's book outside someone's upstairs bathroom at
a party where the main attraction is a magician. I felt
light-headed and silly. Before long, we'd be looking for
the Playdough. But, actually, it was more than childish,
the feeling I had. It was truly like going home again,
like returning not only to childhood, but to this person,
this man himself. I knew him from somewhere, his
mouth, the formation of his teeth, the jumpy ner-
vousness of his laugh. It all fit in some ancient context
that I couldn't place.

His name is David Patterson. Thirty-six years ago,
he was my boyfriend. I doubt that I'd ever have recognized him without the benefit of the name, and of course
"Moore" was no help to him at all. He looked like
Sluggo then, not unlike a lot of little boys. His sandy
hair has faded into an anemic bottom-of-the-moat beige.

His nose is longer, too, sharper and more functional now, a feature to be used, rather than the two damp, pink little windows I used to avoid looking into. David always had a cold.

But he was sexy even then, always asking me if I knew how grown-ups "did it," because he did, even if I didn't, and would I like to try it? He was a street-smart, savvy kid whom nothing phased, least of all the Facts of Life, possibly as a result of growing up around animals. He and his mother lived in an apartment over the garage on Carter's farm. The place smelled of hamsters, which were always getting loose, and old newspapers. David had the biggest comic-book collection the world has ever known, which is probably why I picked Sluggo as his lookalike.

We finished *Small Pig*, and went back downstairs and took possession of a bottle of Beaujolais. We had three and a half decades to catch up on. By the time we got to the last decade, we had had a change of venue, as it were, and, taking advantage of the kids' absence, found ourselves at my house. (I still have trouble saying that to you, *my house*.)

By about 2 A.M., all those years had evaporated, and I felt as if we were back on Carter's farm, doing "the dirty stuff," as we used to call it, in the hayloft. This is how it used to work: I got five strokes, and then he got five, and then I got ten, and then he got ten. I hasten to point out that I always thought, running my finger up and down this little stick that reminded me of asparagus, that girls got the better deal here. Boys had something to show, and that something took several different forms, and could do different things. The best thing was that it could go to the bathroom in the woods without making a mess or having to get undressed. That's *real* penis envy, in my book. When you're on a highway, forty-six miles from a service area, and you see a guy pulled off to the side of the road, standing with his back to the traffic and his head bowed in an attentive, almost reverent manner, you can just feel the relief flowing out with the arc of his water. Those fifteen strokes, in 1950, was as far as *that* went. Not because it was 1950, but because we wanted to move on to the main event, which was to see who could make the broadest jump down out of the hayloft.

Last Saturday we played by our old rules at first. I may have been more game at eight, less eager to please than to be pleased. Yet you'd have thought I did this sort of thing every day. I was uncharacteristically *in* the moment, not holding a mirror up to my performance, much too intrigued to worry about how gross I must look in this position, or that position. Nor did any of my usual compulsions come to haunt me. I don't even know—this may surprise you—if the door was closed or not. None of it was what I imagined making love to another man would be like after all this. I expected to be filled with anxiety, even of shame. But it was gentle, friendly, and safe. Once you were the one I felt safe with, the one who loved me unconditionally, with all my apparent and inapparent imperfections, the one whose love was long-term and transcended the petty, narrow grievances of ordinary people. And now we've come to this, that the very notion of going to bed with you makes me tremble with uncertainty, like baring myself in front of a masked bandit.

AUGUST 5

I'm not sure I like having our children bear witness to my second adolescence. Annie tells her friends on the phone, "My mom's *dating* someone," with a sarcastic emphasis on the word "dating." Annie tends to have a sarcastic emphasis on so many of her words lately, you'd think it would be hard to distinguish. For those special words reserved for upper-case sarcasm, however, she actually lightens the volume, and gives a singsong cadence to the word or phrase. For instance, she's not accustomed to seeing me wear makeup. So, instead of asking me why I don't wear a little makeup, she elevates the heinousness of the crime by saying, in a slightly higher than normal, oh so superior voice, "Hmm, I see we're wearing *just* a little makeup."

She makes me feel ridiculous. But not ridiculous enough. I refrain from scrubbing my face to its formerly squeaky-clean, hormonally repressed condition on the grounds that I've improved upon the essential inadequacy of the basic product.

Annie was at home the night that David and I had our first official date. I wasn't ready, which (unfairly) left Annie to answer the door, Dickens at her side, like an armed guard. As a matter of fact, I have to give Annie a lot of credit. She hates this whole business, and yet finds it in her heart to feed me a few crumbs of support. While I was finishing drying my hair, she bounced into the bathroom to say, "He's kind of cute, Mom."

Peter is less generous. On the few occasions that David has been to the house since then, Peter is hospitable to the extent that he has been willing to look at him, not directly, but sideways, sliding his eyes into the furthermost reaches of their sockets, without moving his head. As far as speaking is concerned, he is brief but conclusive. "Not really" and "Yup" are the collected, unabridged comments made by Peter thus far.

To accept David, or any man that his mother dates, is to betray you. So he feels guilty, and then he's resentful because he's been put in the position of being guilty. As I've said, it would have been easier if you'd died.

But since you're still alive, David and I are careful not to be caught lingering within a radius of one and a half feet of each other. Conversations are stilted, to say the least. In our determination to be innocent, we're all sounding like a bad episode of "Father Knows Best." Better not to appear to know each other too well. I try to remember in Peter's presence, for instance, to ask David whether he takes anything in his coffee. He, in turn, pretends he doesn't remember where I keep the sugar.

I have a problem, I see, being perceived as a sexual person in the eyes of my children. Mothers don't have sex organs; they have birth canals, and these are sewn up and hermetically sealed after the babies are born. Only in emergencies, and with a special note from one's doctor, can the seal be broken.

Just because kids know deep down inside that their parents have sex doesn't make it any less revolting. And then to think that their mother's or father's middle-aged flesh may commingle voluntarily, perhaps even hungrily, with that of some other father or mother is just too much to bear.

Nothing is happening in this house that isn't happening all over America. Why that doesn't make it any easier, I don't know. We haven't even got a good working vocabulary. Peter had his own date the other night. He brought her home after a concert. David was just leaving, so we convened in front of the house.

"Julie, this is my mother," says Peter. "And this is my mother's boyfriend."

No further identification was called for as far as Peter was concerned. Like a name. But the relationship of this man to his mother had to be categorized at once. Must we trot out the nomenclature for any person who happens by? Peter has indicated that he's not particularly interested in this young woman, who is a terribly tall, somewhat vacuous version of Jessica Lang. I doubt he'll see her again. I don't know her last name, or where she lives or goes to school or how she comes to know our son. But she has met a man who has been definitively identified as Peter's mother's boyfriend. And with all— or as little—as that word, *boyfriend*, implies, she has folded that information into her head and taken it home with her.

A U G U S T   1 6

I have just bought all new underwear. Ahem. *Lingerie.*
Nothing like a little romance to boost morale, don't you
agree? Every woman I know has a horror of being struck
by a car and carted off to the hospital, her underwear
to be spread out on a gurney and inspected under the
antiseptic glow of a five-million-watt bulb. And yet
that horror isn't somehow quite enough to send her
scurrying off to Saks Fifth Avenue in search of something more palatable than her own graying cotton as-
sortment with the stretched elastic and the little holes
opening up along the seams. So much more pleasant to
picture the occasional pubic hair poking through a silky
layer of ecru lace. Still: One doesn't quite make it to the
store. Love and only love pushes a woman toward the
ultimate purchase.

"I wouldn't buy it for myself," is what a woman
says. But when it's for him—that's something else. Men
say it, too, in their way. I now recall some purchases of
your own, back in '83 and '84. They were slipped, without comment, into your drawer, spanking new briefs,
bikini briefs, in navy and turquoise and black. This from
the Prince of Deprivation, the man who was philosophi-
cally opposed to throwing away a T-shirt until its neck
was literally severed from the rest of it. My blindness at
the time continues to astound. But if time has done
nothing to lessen my humiliation, I have at least developed an appreciation for the skill with which one can
self-protect. I would say my powers of denial were noth-

ing short of deft. On some magical level, I knew I was
not up to the truth. Indeed, the truth has served me far
better after the fact.

A U G U S T   2 8

For more than four days I have been absolutely alone.
The house is quiet, with a deadly, almost profound,
stillness. I used to laugh about the rabbi who said that
life begins when the children go off to college and the
dog dies. Now I'm less amused.

Only a short while ago, I know, I was complaining.
Make up your mind, you say. *You can't have it both ways.*

I don't think of myself as a woman who's dependent
on her family for an identity, but it was useful having
an ironclad reason to get up in the morning. Cold or
headache or sleepless night, there was no excuse. I was
needed. Deadlines could be missed; the world could wait
for my words. But my daughter could not go off to
school without breakfast, or without lunch in her book
bag, and a kiss; without knowing that her mother was
up and shuffling about, doing her most important job.
Even on their worst days, kids do something vitally
important for their parents. They give them structure,
a place to belong.

They say that people who live alone "get funny."
I'm afraid of getting funny, of being a fringe person,
like a character (how ironic) in one of Esther's favorite
novels. One day, I'll be one of those people I see walking
down the street in a too-small sweater and non-matching
socks, muttering to herself. I'll have what the kids call

"bed head" and an eleven-year-old bottle of ketchup in an otherwise empty refrigerator.

Of course, in my so-called "Twilight Years" I'll have Nina. We have a standing agreement that when the men in our lives have died off, we're going to get adjoining rooms at Wrinklewood, where, as the most notorious eccentrics among our aged fellow retirees, we will stroll around holding hands and wearing the matching sundresses that we bought one year by sheer coincidence.

Nina's greatest fear is that Stephen will be dead, I'll be remarried to someone who eats only bean curd and rice and who will therefore live forever, and she'll have to go to Wrinklewood by herself.

SEPTEMBER 20

I should know better than to complain to Nina about anything. She always tells me the truth. Now I ask you, what kind of a friend is that?

I had been whining once too often about money, about trying to keep this house together, pay the mortgage, come up with the six-month premium on my car insurance, all while writing my November column, about "Our Money" as the great marital illusion. As you know, I never thought there was any such thing as *our* money. There was only *our* money when I wanted to buy something with *my* money. Otherwise, *our* money was *your* money.

But Nina's reached her saturation point on the subject. "*Why* don't you just face facts and rent out part of your house? You don't need all those rooms, and taking in even one boarder would make your life so much easier."

Nina can't stand anyone who lets herself be victimized. Never have I ever heard Nina say, "I don't know what to do." More to the point, I've never heard her say, "I don't know what you should do." She knows exactly what I should do and when I should do it. She can be wrong, mind you. She can make big mistakes, usually by moving too quickly. Like a lot of small, wiry people, Nina's incapable of doing anything in a leisurely way, so why should it be any different when it comes to opening her mouth? She's been known to offend several of her closest friends in a single afternoon. But she speaks her mind, and the solution is immediately clear to her.

I, on the other hand, am more of a plodder. I think about things, chew them around in my head for a while. I'm a ruminant, basically, grazing over the landscape, taking in a little of this and a little of that. What I find is that there's a bit of the inedible in every patch.

I always hear myself saying, "yes, but," when I talk to Nina. Yes, but what do I do when Annie and Peter come home from college? Yes, but I want privacy; yes, but I don't want a complete stranger bumping into me in the hallway at night; yes, but I don't want someone else's groceries in my refrigerator.

"Yes, but you don't have enough money," she says.

Yes, but—I just want to complain. It's true I can rent a couple of rooms. It's true I can get more money. What I can't do is alter the fact that life at this stage, according to that rabbi, is not the way my life appears to be headed. *Life begins when the kids go off to college and the dog dies and you take in a boarder.* I don't think so.

OCTOBER 7

The leaves are curling on the horse chestnut; the cicadas are dropping from the trees; dark closes in on my late-afternoon walks with Dickens. It all spells fall, and you leaving. Up the street, someone lights a fire. The smell of it wafts across my consciousness like a broken promise, and there you are. God, but associations are slow to die.

It's been just over a year since you left to sleep on a futon. I knew then that I had lost my husband. It had been my husband who had gone; and one day, perhaps, it would be my husband who would return. But the man I did not count on losing, did not think about then, was my best friend. I mourned for my marriage, but I forgot to mourn for my friend. He's the one I miss the most.

The man who was my husband dates another woman; I date another man. We come and go, each of us, to movies, and to dinner, and to bed. It's nice. I'm okay. You don't need to feel guilty anymore. But where, I wonder, even in the middle of a great sunny Sunday morning, when the maple tree outside my window is an explosion of yellow and David is on his way over to see me, where is that friend I used to have, the one with the dark, soulful eyes and the kinky hair who used to spin out his insane ideas over a second cup of coffee? Where is he who listened attentively to my endless, groundless, neurotic fears and wound up actually convincing me that they were functions of creativity? When was the moment that he ceased to think of me not only as his lover, but also as his friend?

All those past joys and certainties have been negated, erased. The intimacies that wove us together have come unraveled like an old blanket that somebody left on a park bench. And there is nothing, nothing in this life that can replace them. How does one unlearn one's past?

So it wasn't the marriage I took for granted all these years; it was, I have been slow to see, the friendship I could not imagine being without. It's our imagination that has failed us, so much we did not, could not, picture. You said once on the telephone, "If either of us gets married again—" And stopped yourself, asking, "I can't imagine that, can you?"

"No," I said. "But then there are a lot of things I couldn't imagine."

OCTOBER 26

Trust me when I tell you, she almost got the lamb chops. What a sweet scene, Isabel skipping down the aisles of Corelli's, looking positively radiant from the nip in the air and the excitement of preparing a special dinner for you while I, the knowing ex-wife-elect, peer into her shopping basket, nodding approval.

I smiled. She smiled. I could see us in a comic strip, balloons of words forming over our heads. *Hmm, sausage, lamb chops, looks like a mixed grill; why, of course, it's his birthday, and she's cooking his favorite dinner. She sees me looking, knows I know. I wonder if she'll select an alternative menu. A new lover hardly wants to trail along in the path of her predecessor.*

Isabel, meanwhile: *She knows it's his birthday, it's probably the same damn dinner she's given him since he was twenty-five. I wonder if he'd really mind that much if I got something else . . .* When I saw her again at the checkout counter, the lamb chops had been replaced by Cornish hens. Separations would be so dull, wouldn't they, without these unexpected encounters? It was like looking into a room that had been vacated after I'd gone. It was your next life. I'd label it, *After Emily*.

N O V E M B E R 5

Three days ago, a man told me that my body was a work of art. I liked that: *A work of art.* The man was David, but what I'm still trying to absorb is that an actual man, someone with reasonably good eyesight, feels that way about me. There was a time when such an idea would have seemed hilarious. In college I went out with someone whose mother pulled him aside one parents' weekend after she had met me, and said, "Someday, John, you and your brother are going to realize that there's more to life than a blond body." What a bizarre way to describe a woman whose body was only slightly less seductive than that of an eleven-year-old boy. Even my boyfriend got a lot of mileage out of that, addressing me in front of his fraternity brothers as, "Inga from the Land of the Big Knockers and The Midnight Sun."

I seem to have come a long way, baby, as they say, at least as far as the body is concerned. But I'm still at the stage when everything David says or does comes across in a historical context, thrown into relief against the background of the past. He can't open his mouth without my thinking, *Would Nick have said that?* In this instance, I think I can safely assume that the answer is no. *I'm leaving my wife. She has a body like a work of art.* It doesn't quite fit, does it?

We took so much for granted, Nick. Maybe that was our biggest mistake. I think of how disdainful I was of my mother when, at the end of the day, she would brush her teeth and powder her nose and put on more lipstick before my father came home. It didn't matter what she had been doing, whether she herself had only just come home from work, or whether she'd been pulling crabgrass. My father's imminent arrival would make its way into her consciousness, and she would pop in front of the mirror to set about preparing herself for him.

This effort my mother made to make herself attractive to my father at all times infuriated me. I saw it as deferential, demeaning; I thought she lacked the confidence just to *be*. Did she think he wouldn't love her with a single hair out of place, or with dirt under her fingernails? And if he didn't, what of it? What did that make him? Surely, I thought, if she went about her business, if she didn't cater to him, he might love her more; he might love her more than she knew.

So what am I saying? Maybe that I might have tried harder to let you know that I cared whether I was attractive to you. I might have made an effort to convey to you how lucky I was to have you come home at the end of the day. Who knows all I might have done, if I could have done anything at all.

We could spend the rest of our lives thinking of all the what if's. It's certainly my kind of preoccupation. In the meantime, I'm reveling in being regarded as a work of art. It's like having someone pull me out of the back of a closet and dust me off to discover that— wow!—I'm an original, a museum piece. I wouldn't want to call in any experts on this. No second opinions, please! I'm not asking any questions, not thinking about where this will lead. I'm just going to lie in my bed in the morning, stretch with the sunrise, and feel the blood return. I'm going to savor the sensation of having my body come back to life, hungry inch by hungry inch.

NOVEMBER 11

You must have heard that Harvey and June are getting separated. I'm upset; you don't know how much I've counted on them. They've taught me how to laugh even when it isn't funny—*mainly* when it isn't funny. I've always adored that about the Littles. When they're at their most impoverished, with creditors knocking on the door and making threatening phone calls, that's when you'll find them doubled over laughing because they'd just received an invitation to open up a charge account at Saks Fifth Avenue.

We've been each other's best audience, though I
hope I won't have any more of Harvey's telephone so-
licitations for the home for unwed mothers. He's always
so convincing, affecting that soft, angelic voice with the
slight speech impediment. *If you could justh contribute
a thmall amount, anything at all, it would be thoo much
apprethiated.*

And then, when I've made my excuses, *Well, Jesuth
Critht, if you can't give anything for God . . .*

How can a couple who has separated three times
not be together? I suppose it would shock a lot of people
to know that Harvey and June didn't have the ideal
marriage. They have that surface dazzle, like two people
who've just stepped out of an F. Scott Fitzgerald novel.
She laughs at all his funny routines as though hearing
them for the first time; he goes all moist in the eyes
when she steps into a room, as if he's thinking, *This is
my wife; this remarkable specimen is my wife.* Who would
guess that in real life, after the guests go home, they're
Alice and Ralph Kramden?

But, to you and me, that mercurial aspect is precisely what gives them their solidarity. What can they
possibly discover about this process that they don't already know? After all, it was they who begged us, *Don't
do it. It's expensive, and it doesn't solve anything.* I can't bear
to watch. It's like going through it again, like looking in
a mirror and watching it break into small pieces.

NOVEMBER 17

Another season of leaves has fallen in our backyard. It has not escaped me that when we talk property division, this is our house, our five eighths of an acre, our trees— and my leaves. Right about now, I'd like to put some fine-tuning into our joint custody agreements.

I feel like the neighborhood pariah, rustling around knee-deep in reminders of my slovenliness. A lot of the pressure comes, not from the neighbors, who don't know quite what to make of me, but from Dickens, who has trouble keeping track of his toys. He goes galloping through the drifts, his nose to the ground, trying to ferret out his frog, among other things. When he isn't involved in a project, he seems depressed, a dog in need of something to do. He's not eating. This morning, he was asleep with his ear in his water bowl. It was a dead, unproductive sleep, with little rapid eye movement and squirrel chasing. I don't think he likes this life. It's pointless and disorienting. Dickens reminds me of the Littles' cat, who went on a hunger strike when June changed her job and started commuting to New York, adding four hours to her workday. Remember the vet's report after two weeks of observation? *Will eat lobster if fed by hand.*

I expected, by now, to be headed in some definitive direction—either we'd be getting divorced, or we'd be trying to reconcile. Maybe I'm being arbitrary, but I think that after a year's time, we should have a game plan. I'm not good at holding my life in abeyance. We don't seem to be taking another look at this marriage; nor are we making a commitment to the new people in our lives. How can we? A "trial separation," we called it. What it is is a long, open-ended recess and, for my part, I've tried to make the most of it. But we've been out on the playground too long. What's happened is that it has become easier to stay out here than it is to face going back inside, where there's work to be done.

Several months ago, I sat on your futon, listening to you tick off the reasons why you began your affair with Esther. It all added up to my fault. I'll take my share of the blame. But I'm tired of being told that I wasn't a grown-up, that I was the child and you were the adult. Because it seems to me, while you're being so grown up, that you might take some responsibility for what you've done. I wasn't so childish way back in the early seventies, when we were busy sitting in circles, passing around these soggy joints and having an "open marriage" in our bell-bottoms, that I didn't realize I needed to do something for myself, and for us, by going into therapy. It would not have occurred to me to list all the reasons why what I was doing was your fault.

If you're paying me back, if that's what this is all about, I'd like to remind you that the statute of limitations has run out on those particular offenses. They have been behind us for nearly fifteen years. We can't change any of that. The point is who we are today, and what we want to do about it.

NOVEMBER 30

Now I can give thanks—that it's over. Even for tradi-
tional families, Thanksgiving can be hell. My parents
always played hosts to warring great-aunts who, sometime before dinner and after the second manhattan,
would square off in front of the stove and rekindle some
family feud that had been going on for thirty years.

My mother's mother, meanwhile, would be sitting
by the fire in the living room, trying to deflect the ten-
sion by giving anyone within hearing distance a tour of
her charm bracelet. Between points of interest, we were
aware of the muffled growls of dispute that inevitably
erupted between my aunt and uncle, who managed
never to take the same train home. But with all that, a
generous spirit survived. We fell into bed exhausted and
amused. When we awoke in the morning, all was well.

For twenty years, you and I carried on this tradition, with all of its attendant generational and culinary
conflicts, i.e., the annual canned-versus-homemade
cranberry-sauce controversy, over which certain people
threatened not to make an appearance at dinner. The
house echoes with all those creaky, cranky voices we'd
have loved to silence with the wave of a wooden spoon.
Today, I'd bring them back in a flash.

Thanksgiving is a time of togetherness. It wasn't
meant for people who don't know what to do with
their marriages. It wasn't meant for people who have
boyfriends over forty, and whose children say things
like, "I suppose your *boyfriend's* coming for dinner." I

don't know about you, but while we're keeping our options open, I occasionally glance at my plate to see that there's nothing on it. I think it's time we served up a little decision.

As it happens, my "boyfriend" did not come for dinner. David and Audrey, his soon-to-be ex-wife, are still keeping up the pretense of unity for their youngest son, who is only eight. I don't know if I've mentioned Barney. If not, it's probably because, like David himself, I can't quite believe that there's someone that young in my life. David didn't think it necessary to talk about Barney until I walked into his apartment for the first time and saw the bunk beds. "Who gets the top?" I asked, a sudden, awful realization seeping into my brain.

"The guest gets to pick," he said. "Those are the house rules."

"How old is he?" I asked, hearing my voice break. "The host, I mean."

His face grew serious. "I was afraid to tell you, and then I couldn't tell you, because I hadn't told you."

Barney's a terrific kid, but I don't know what to say to an eight-year-old anymore, to say nothing of an eight-year-old who's a genius and likes to build telescopes in his spare time and who says he doesn't like school because it doesn't give him time to think.

Barney was brought into this world to save his parents' marriage. He was the human equivalent of a new addition on a house, a new swimming pool, or a tennis court, that second wind, a bellows bearing a banner: *We still have a future.*

It's a mission no child deserves, although if anyone were up to the task, it would be Barney. He's a real sparkler, but I appreciate him from afar, like a newly discovered planet. He stays with David every other week, which means that David has to drive him to school out in Bryn Mawr. And where does that leave me on those weeks? Mostly, shuffling around my office/house, trying to find some delineation between the end of the day and the evening, some sign that work is over and it's time to go home. Usually I wind up celebrating that period of time with a glass of wine and Jim Lehrer and Robin MacNeil on the NewsHour. But now and then, if I'm good, I get invited to go with David and Barney to Roy Rogers!

DECEMBER 18

This might be one of those scenes in which the wife is sitting in a rocking chair with her needles and a ball of knitting, a knowing little Mona Lisa smile on her face. The husband has just come home from work, having plopped his hat on the hall table, and she's about to tell him a joyful little piece of news.

I say *might* be one of those scenes. Except that I have no husband to speak of, no hat on the hall table, no knitting. What I do have are bad vibes brought to me by a wall calendar that is beginning to look more and more like 1963, when I shared my apartment with three other women who were, on occasion, late with their periods. The calendar was so filled with calculations, you couldn't see what day it was, or even what year.

Three little letters tell the whole story. LMP. Re-

member them? Probably not. It's been a long time. They
stand for Last Menstrual Period, or, in this case, November 2.

How, you might ask, does one get into such a
situation at this, uh, mature age? I don't know. "I didn't
think I was very fertile anymore," doesn't sound like
much of an answer, does it? And yet it's the truth.
"Very," however, may be the operational word. At any
rate, it's a highly humiliating position I'm in. Besides
which, having falsely presented myself as a responsible,
intelligent person for the last twelve years, I can hardly
go to my regular doctor.

Time was when our doctors were the priests of our
lives, pillars of the community. That trust, for many,
has eroded; but not for me. If Dr. John Altar of Boston
still lives, I would sooner die than return to him in the
same nervous condition that first took me to him in the
early sixties. I had found his name, as one might guess,
in the yellow pages. What a boon to his practice his
name must have been.

I had never been examined by an obstetrician/gyne-
cologist before. But his office, far from imposing, had
at least some superficial warmth: wooden filing cabinets,
cheerful curtains on the windows, prints of old Boston.
Lurking in the corners, though, were these things, plastic models in an angry Pepto Bismol pink, drawings of
fetuses, shiny metal instruments, stirrups. I thought I
might be sick. I didn't know how my body worked,
didn't want to know, didn't want anyone else to know.
All those things that my mother used to store in her
night table—rubber disks, a long black hook shaped like
a small spine with ridges, petrolatum-based jellies. The

mere word "petrolatum" was disgusting, like "unguent," and brought to mind unsavory substances. You
couldn't pay me to walk into a drugstore and say, "I'll
have a tube of this rectal unguent."

I didn't even really know what sex was, not yet. It
had nothing to do with children. I was still learning how
to be womanly. Dr. Altar was a grandfatherly sort of
man who kept his judgments, if he had any, to himself.

What a shame, he said softly, that it takes only once.
Was I planning to marry the young man?

We had talked of getting married, "the young man"
and I. But not in those last few weeks. In those last few
weeks, I had been a woman ahead of her times, doing
all the pursuing, all the telephoning. From the minute
he said hello, his disappointment was palpable, his conversation monosyllabic and awkward. The more he
seemed to withdraw, the more I advanced, piling humiliation upon humiliation. My face still burns from the
memory of that time.

Dr. Altar sat me down after the examination and
reassured me as best he could. He did not believe that I
was pregnant, though it was too early to be sure. I went
back to my apartment and waited to prove him right.

Three days later, I bled richly, triumphantly, onto
the back of my camel-hair skirt. I was at work, of
course. But the gods had been kind, and such is the sort
of price one pays for the small, reckless prayers, the deal
of a sinner, whispered on her knees at a desperate hour.

I was lucky, then. So much luckier than Margot,
my office crony, whose friends all chipped in so that she
could travel to Newark to see a nurse, a woman whose

name was known by a woman who was known by another woman who had once needed an abortion. The procedure was simple. And very nearly deadly. On the plane on the way home, she began hemorrhaging. Her parents, a crusty, fragile couple in their sixties, were summoned to Boston City Hospital. What had happened to their daughter was incomprehensible because Margot, the baby of the family, had always been such a good girl. From then on, Margot was treated with polite indifference, as if she were invisible. And she was never able to have children.

Twenty-two years later, a woman can escape. I've had my children. I'm acting within the law. The long-term consequences are small. I don't know what it is, then, that makes me unspeakably sad.

1986

The doctor had a middle-European accent and an unpro-
nounceable name with lots of y's. I was obstinate in my
refusal to learn it, spell it, own it in any permanent way,
as part of my memory, my life.

He was an attractive man, and polite, but to the
point. I was, he said, about six weeks pregnant. I was
forty-four, with two grown children. Probably, I did
not wish to have the child, was that correct?

Correct, indeed. I had heard that he was not a hand-
holder. That was okay. This was not a difficult decision;
I would not grieve for what might have been. What was
difficult was accepting in myself the failings that had
brought me to his office in the first place. I didn't know
what to call them, specifically, but I had been careless,
possibly even defiant. And let's not forget stupid. Pregnant is something one's adolescent children become by
mistake. Besides which, abortion, however you feel
about the right to choose, is ugly, demeaning. Both of
us found it personally abhorrent, so you and I were
exceedingly cautious after we had Annie so as never to
be faced with that decision.

I wanted to get it over with, that minute, if I could.
Knowing there was something in my body that I didn't
want, and that it was growing, was making me crazy.
But it would be nearly a week before anything could be
scheduled. Unfortunately, Peter and Annie were still at
home. I wasn't exactly at my best, falling asleep at about
seven-thirty at night, and gagging over the butter melting on an English muffin in the morning. Sometimes
I'd succeed in fighting it back, swallowing waves of

black bile. I'd have done anything rather than face the revulsion Annie and Peter would have felt if they'd had any inkling that their mother was pregnant.

Another thing was that my editor wanted a column about laughing in bed. We tossed this around on the phone one afternoon as I was chomping on a stack of Saltines. She wanted a supportive, funny piece about a sudden, stabbing leg cramp, say, while trying a new position. I was blocked on the subject. The one position I envisioned with any clarity was dry heaving over a toilet bowl.

All this while making preparations for my "procedure." David was going to take me to the hospital, wait for me, and drive me home when it was over. He's a problem-solver, a doer. And he was doing all the right things. I needed him, and he wasn't going to let me down. But he's not a talker. I was having trouble getting an accurate reading on how he felt about this, or anything else, for that matter. The relationship was interesting, puzzling, because of what wasn't said. I knew how I felt. I felt that there was something important missing; that I liked him; that I loved many things about him, his complete and uncompromised love of children, his boyishness, his spontaneity, his imagination, his humor, his lustiness. It was a sexy relationship in that it worked. David was a good lover, technically; he had been a good student of sex. But there was a feeling, overall, perhaps because of our history together, of two children at play. We made love the way we ate, with appetite but without passion. It filled us up temporarily, like a really good bowl of creamed soup.

I was about to say that we were like brother and

sister, but it was less personal than that. Brothers and sisters have a loyalty that abides. They understand each other in ways that no other person can. The truth was that I had been so eager to be reconnected, so eager to make my life whole again, that I didn't notice the lack of intimacy. Having someone to love was a salve rather than a solution. To David, I could just as easily have been any other woman that he found attractive. I was but one of numerous works of art. With little inconvenience to him I could be replaced.

It wasn't just a lack of intimacy that bothered me; there was a lack of complexity. David doesn't like to dig, or speculate, hypothesize, or analyze. He has a black-and-white way of translating his world. Happy, unhappy. Good movie, bad movie. Fun, not fun. I could just see him pinning the latter label on dealing with my abortion and tacking it on the wall of his brain for future reference.

Friends who have had abortions tell me they didn't know what grief was until then. They cry on the way home. They cry for a month. Two months. Three months. *You'll get over it,* they're told.

I did not cry on the way home. I was a good sport, bleeding cheerfully, resolutely, into a sanitary pad the size of a mattress. But it was just that: being a good sport, not being complicated, not letting all the gray show, made me feel lonely when I was with David.

Babies had been coming and going through the lobby when I was waiting to register at the outpatient desk. I didn't want a baby. What I wanted was the certainty that I saw in the young mothers' faces as they carried these bundles in their arms: *This is what I want, my baby, I have what I want.* I had been one of those mothers, once, I was certain. I had what I wanted, I had Annie and Peter. They were like the sun. Now I don't know what I want.

I know only what I don't want. I don't want a husband who doesn't want me. I don't want a husband who lies, a husband who has a problem for which he then finds a solution that he then keeps secret.

Nor do I want to be with a man who's only there for the good times. I want to be cared for, nurtured. Everything in David's life shows signs of neglect. If I bring flowers to put on the table, they are left until they die and the water turns green. The blossoms drop over the edge of the vase as if they'd been shot in the back. I don't want to be just one more flower that dies on the table without notice.

I don't want to be with someone who knows how to eat, but not how to dine. David doesn't cook; he heats. Leftover pizza, frozen dinners, stromboli, and ravioli.

Nor, much as I like Barney, do I want an eight-year-old boy for an alternate-week companion. I think my Little League days are over. And while I'm busy with the elimination process, Dr. Bloom reminds me that if I don't want a, b, or c, I'll get something else. I'll get what's left over.

So here I am, in a spanking-new year, feeling a bit sober, empty. The abortion was, literally, a purge. My insides have been sucked out. "You'll feel a tug," the doctor had said. "A cramp." I pictured the wall of my uterus being pulled, like the hem of a bedspread, into the hose of a vacuum cleaner.

Now that I've been hollowed out, I need to put something back, something wholesome, that will feel good. You can't pick up where you left off. You can't just get rid of the baby and go back to being lovers, not unless you want to use the experience as something unfortunate but necessary between you, not unless you want to smooth it down and build upon it, like a foundation. We were not building. We were sidestepping, a day at a time. I knew that it was over, but I was grateful to David since, though he didn't realize it at the time, he taught me something important.

It was one of the first nights we had the house to ourselves. Barney was with his mother that week, and Annie was with friends. I remember that it was a Thursday, because we were going to get in bed and watch "Hill Street Blues." David got into the bed and spread his arms out wide, as if to circumscribe his territory. "This," he said, "this is the first thing you have to learn to do when you get separated. You have to learn to move to the middle of the bed." All the while as I lay there for the next hour, as people ran in and out of the police station and telephones rang and I got caught up in these parallel dramas, I was smiling to myself with the simplicity of that notion: *Move to the middle of the bed*. It was a metaphor so obvious that one might almost be embarrassed to mention it out loud.

J A N U A R Y   3 1

The other day, when the space shuttle Challenger and its crew scattered into eternity, I was practicing the fundamentals of cross-country skiing out on the golf course. When I learned it had happened, I was seated across from my mother in a restaurant, going over the luncheon menu.

"I suppose you've heard," she said in a disheartened way. But I hadn't heard. She gave me a look, at once amazed and appalled.

I thought, then, without words equal to the moment, of all the postponements, of all the times I had stayed tuned, knowing that with that kind of meticulous attention, that kind of caution, nothing could go wrong. "Her children were watching," my mother said, referring to Scott and Caroline McAuliffe. The waitress came to take our orders. She was cheerful, engaging, efficient. If she knew anything that happened at Cape Canaveral, there was no sign of it.

All afternoon it was like that. In Florida and elsewhere, those who had watched the launching, either live or on television, were coming out of shock to mourn; I ate a platter of chicken salad and fried oysters. My mother and I had no further discussion about Christa McAuliffe and the astronauts and their families. On the way home, I stopped at the dry cleaner's to pick up a blouse and was told to have a nice day.

Minutes later, I was watching Dan Rather and replays of the liftoff. I heard the countdown—and the silence. Then, tearfully, Ronald Reagan began to speak. Before he had finished, the phone rang. It was the receptionist in my gynecologist's office, confirming my appointment for the next day.

Vaginas, I thought. *How could she be thinking about vaginas? How could I have eaten a platter of chicken and oysters and remembered to pick up the blouse?*

Yet, in a funny way, it was reassuring that there were these ordinary things to consider. I remember what Lydia had said, in *Disturbances in the Field,* after her two youngest children were killed in a bus accident: that she kept thinking a time would come when she could look at a chartered bus without feeling sick; when she could look at snow falling, or pass a school group on the street, when all these ordinary things would resume their rightful proportions and places in a universe of ordinary things.

Perhaps, at a time when a tragedy is the last thing we think of before we go to sleep and first thing we think of when we wake up in the morning, the ordinary is our refuge.

Occasionally, in the last couple of days, I've thought about what must be going through the minds of the eleven thousand other people who had applied for Christa McAuliffe's position. But mostly I've done what I've always done—talked with friends about the flu and about the movies and parking tickets. I shoveled the walk. I thought about us, and about Peter and Annie; I wished they weren't so far away. I read "Doonesbury" and "Cathy." While across the country flags fly at half-mast, Cathy's been busy accusing her best friend, who's getting married, of desertion.

On Wednesday night, the *MacNeil/Lehrer News-Hour* devoted its entire program to Challenger and to events nationwide following the explosion. Among the numerous people interviewed was a former astronaut by the name of Deke Slayton, who said flatly that if something happens, "You can't fix it. Get on with it—that's the right stuff."

Certainly it's the message of the hour, that beyond these events something abides. We do get on with it. We let ordinary things resume their rightful proportions and places in a universe of ordinary things. It's both the amazing thing and the sad thing that we do.

F E B R U A R Y   1 1

It seems whenever a man leaves a woman, the first thing she does is join an exercise class. I'm no exception. I sign up for ten weeks, go to a few classes until I feel a little better, and then I stop. I'm there just long enough to remember why I quit, which is that I hate working on my body, and to find out what the current fashion is in the fitness world. Leotards and leg warmers are out, as I learned yesterday.

I'd have sooner died than have you know this at the time, but back in 1984, when part of my game plan was to make you regret what you had done by metamorphosing into a perfect 10—and not incidentally, to improve my marketability—I joined a serious exercise class that was full of serious people who knew that old T-shirts and sweatpants were passé. So I bought a pair of aerobic shoes, tights, a leotard, leg warmers, and a pair of warm-up pants. There was a problem, however, when I got up to go to class the next morning: I seemed to have an excess of clothing. Or, looking at it another way, too few legs. I didn't know whether to put my leg warmers on over my tights and under my warm-up pants, or put my warm-up pants on over my tights and put the leg warmers on last. Fortunately, there was a certain adolescent on hand for critical comment.

Annie was trying to be patient. "Mom," she said, "if you have leg warmers, you don't need warm-up pants."

I was crushed. Not need warm-up pants? They were the most serious item of all. I had to wear them; I'd spent all this money. I was *committed*. "Well, Mo-om," she said. "Go ahead and wear them, then. And carry the leg warmers over your arm." In all my years of watching people run and dance and do exercises, I had never seen anyone carry her leg warmers, but I was too late to argue. As I remember, the class was half over before I got the shoes off, the leg warmers on, and the shoes back on again. It was like trying to get into your snowsuit while everyone else is out at recess already. You'd think I'd have learned something.

Not so. Now I'm back to getting purple in the face and pretending that a pulse of two hundred and eighty beats a minute is normal, that I'm not going to drop dead while wearing the obligatory long old T-shirt, as opposed to the short old T-shirt, and these sexy leggings that end at the ankles. In every manner of speaking, I can't keep up.

To My Ex-Husband

Heartbreak is when you get a handmade valentine from the child of the man you're no longer seeing. I was okay until then. I was okay until Barney let it be known that he was part of this thing, too. Nina said, "You mean he didn't know that you'd broken up?"

"It was worse than that," I said. "He knew."

It also happened to be one of the most beautiful valentines I'd ever received. It was a collage, a black cardboard heart on which he'd pasted half of a smaller heart made of perfectly gorgeous shiny wrapping paper, silver on one side, red on the other. He'd folded it down the center, so when you open it up there are all these little pieces, like washers and nuts, that look as if they're from the inside of a faucet glued on in the shape of a heart. On the bottom, he'd written, "You make things come together."

I had been so self-absorbed that I had not considered how this would affect him. I don't know about David; but Barney certainly deserves better than that.

Nina, eager to keep me from self-destructing, recruited me to help her with a restaurant review. "Would you mind?" she asks. Would I *mind*? Who's she kidding? Since when have matters of the heart ever interfered with my appetite, especially at one of what is known in the business as a "deep-pocket" restaurant?

I have to finally concede, however, that this job isn't all about eating. It's about adjectives. How many different words can one find to describe the flavor of a dish? Nina, at least, does not resort to words like "honest," nor pay tribute to veal stocks that have "integrity."

The deal is that each of you orders enough food for four, plus every dessert on the menu. Then you sample each one. I'm sure these places must get suspicious. I always expect to find Nina slipping into the restaurant looking like Miss Piggy as the Underground Restaurant Critic, in a huge hat tipped down over one eye and sunglasses with lenses the size of a satellite dish.

By the time I got to the lush white-chocolate mousse set on a thin disk of dark chocolate awash in a pool of fresh raspberry sauce and covered with lacy threads of hardened caramel, I had almost, *almost*, forgotten the difficulties of the last weeks. It hadn't been fun. But perhaps I had paved the way for that to come.

MARCH 5

I gave in, finally, to the idea of having a boarder, and called a woman who had put an ad up on the bulletin board of the co-op. The time seemed right, and not only because I was in the position of choosing between my car insurance and groceries—not a tough choice, on the surface, given my attitude toward food. But not having a car represented such a loss of mobility that I was feeling claustrophobic.

The woman was here for two weeks. I liked Valerie, who was about sixty, because she reminded me of Ruth Gordon in *Rosemary's Baby*. She had that same lively and eccentric quality. Also, she was a flutist. I thought I might be lured into playing the piano again;

at least, I might get the thing tuned. The music was a selling point, but she had neglected to mention the hot plate. She would come home late at night from an engagement and do stir-fry. I'd be awakened at all hours of the night, smelling soy sauce, soybeans, soysage (you know, tastes like sausage?). This mixed with ginger and bean curd.

My refrigerator looked like a health-food store. There were compressed pies of yet another form of soy that swelled and oozed out of their casings when you put them in the toaster oven. There were dietary supplements of all kinds, as well as maximum-stress capsules and a giant bottle of a miracle drink that contained, among other things, purified water, caramel color, glycerin, potassium citrate, ferric glycerophosphate, chamomile flower, sarsaparilla root, celery seed, alfalfa herb, dandelion root, horehound herb, licorice root, senega root, passion flower, thyme leaf, gentian root, saw palmetto berry, angelica root, *Cascara sagrada* bark, potassium hydroxide, and vanillin, *plus* artificial flavors. I was glad I wasn't pregnant. She might have forced me to eat the stuff and then send me off to the devil's disciple, Dr. Sapperstein.

I didn't really object to Valerie's using the hot plate, except for the hour that she chose to use it. But it meant that I myself couldn't do much cooking. All the dishes were upstairs, in her bathtub, not that she seemed inclined to wash them.

Then there was the cat, which she had also not mentioned. Charleston—so named because somebody had given him to her when she went down there for a music festival—was good about his litter box, and stayed in her room, where he set about shredding the furniture. Valerie had bought him an upholstered post to climb on, but he much preferred the chairs. All this might have been manageable eventually, but Dickens became obsessed. The minute Charleston moved in, Dickens launched into a twenty-four-hour surveillance program. Day and night you could hear him pacing back and forth, sniffing at the airspace under Valerie's door. I thought I might have to serve him his dinner up there, but after a couple of days he'd take a break, put in a quick appearance at his bowl, and head right back to work, still chewing his kibble on the way.

Valerie was giving me a check for another week when she asked if her boyfriend could rent the other room. I'd met him only once. He was the spitting image of Mr. Hooper on "Sesame Street," which made him a great temptation. But I was getting in over my head, and was hugely relieved to be able to say that I needed the room for Annie. The next day, she and Charleston moved out. Dickens hopped alongside her on two legs as she carried Charleston in his cat-cage down the stairs and out to her car, setting what has to be a record for an ostensibly four-legged beast. I wish David Letterman had been here!

Okay, Nick. I think we should get something straight. I'm a little sick of having it get back to me, especially through the children, that I'm ripping you off by living in luxury in a three-thousand-square-foot house while you're stuck in a one-bedroom apartment. Yes, I complain about the maintenance. I'd be complaining about it if you were here, only there would be two of us working to pay for it. This house is falling apart. The septic system is leaking, the windowsills are rotting, and every month yet another section of the roof has to be repaired. Meanwhile, I'm supposed to feel grateful to you for paying the utilities, something you seem to think makes you a good guy. Well, you need to be educated. If we took this to court, you'd be required to do that and more. But that isn't the biggest problem, as I see it. The biggest problem is that you have a talent for turning everything around so that it fits your image of yourself as an innocent bystander: *Poor Nick. He's so sweet. What did he do to deserve this?*

Let me just remind you of a little something: You left. I'm doing everything I can to stay in this house, including teaching three sections of eighth-grade English while someone is on maternity leave. I do it not merely for the money, but for the unmitigated joy of hearing loudly whispered choruses of "Whack off, Whack off!" from the boys in the back row while I hold forth on the major themes of *The Old Man and the Sea.*

But Nick: The house is the only constancy Annie

and Peter have. I'm not about to divvy it up, in any case, just so that you can feel better knowing that I, too, am living in what used to be referred to as "reduced circumstances." I'm just plain not ready, and I'll tell you something else: Neither is Dickens. It's just no fun jumping up onto a futon.

What's the matter, anyway, that you have to start picking on me again? Aren't things going well with Isabel?

APRIL 22

If I were to write an autobiography, an apt title would be *I Should Have Known.* So. It hasn't worked out with Isabel. I wish I could say that I was sorry. I wish I could say more about what I wish for your happiness. I *do* wish for it. But it hurts me to be excluded from it.

Apart from that, I think that being involved with a woman whose six-year-old son sleeps with her does not portend well for the relationship. Isabel should pack him off now and then with his older brothers. They'll straighten him out. Whose is the greater need here, Isabel's or Andrew's? If it's Isabel's, I have to say that, for warmth and security, a dog is a much safer bet. Of course Dickens doesn't like to share me, but he deals with his feelings constructively, by shredding the edges of the rugs. Unlike Andrew, he doesn't take it out on the men in my life. I understand that he bit you. Now that's what I call feedback. There's no mystery as to where *you* stand.

p.s. I can't help noticing that you seem to surround

yourself with women who have at least one child that is still young. Esther. Isabel. The women in your apartment building—friendly but unromantic attachments. Saturday-night casseroles. Movies. Museums. It's a nesting instinct come late in life. You were hardly at home when Peter and Annie were little. Now you seem to want to replicate the family you're missing. It makes me wonder: If you married a woman who'd never had children, would you have more children? It's a thought that fills me with fascination and horror all at the same time. So many men want to start over. They want to do it *right* this time, like my neighbor's ex-husband. He looks at the daughter he has, the one he wasn't there for. He sees his mistakes. Never mind that she's a perfectly wonderful girl; what he means is that she lacks his imprint. So he undoes his vasectomy and has another child. As this woman said to me, "You know—it's like you throw the first crepe away."

M A Y   1 0

Nina says she ran into you, and you'd heard that I was seeing somebody, "a proctologist, I think."

A proctologist, I think not. He's a periodontist, though for dating purposes it may be a toss-up, one of life's hard choices.

I'd been seeing him (Dr. Ventura) long before I started dating him on a regular basis. "Bloody Wednesdays," I called them. Do you remember my telling you that I was earning extra money teaching? This is one of the reasons. It is the nearly-two-thousand-dollar reason.

But I knew I was in for trouble when my regular dentist stood by my chair, pressing a mini-ruler into my gums and calling out numbers to the hygienist: *eight, nine, ten.* These were otherwise perfectly innocent numbers with pleasant, if sometimes seasonal, associations, like maids-a-milking and ladies dancing. I heard nothing less than a seven, which in the world of dentistry meant I was getting dangerously long in the tooth, and could well have used some twos and threes, some turtle doves and French hens. The solution is to take the patient's mouth, divide it into quadrants, and cut away the loose tissue, thereby tightening the gums around those wobbling teeth.

I don't suppose a dentist normally wants to date his patient any more than a patient wants to date him. My experience has been that the very thought of a dentist makes my eyes water and shifts my salivary glands into overdrive, not for the usual reasons, but because of those sharp pieces of cardboard they stuff into your mouth when they're taking X rays. I wind up gagging, ejecting the thing like a dart, and we have to start all over with the child-sized one.

Yet, much as I dreaded it, it didn't seem like a normal situation from the beginning. I don't know— maybe he (Edward) thought I appeared pitiful. Certainly I wouldn't have made great copy for the personals: *Single, forty-ish female, with financial problems and bleeding gums, seeks curettage, and much, much more.* Anyway, he seemed to genuinely care about my swelling gingiva and their instant pink eruptions at the touch of a toothbrush, seemed to care about my well-being, my children in college, my work, and—this was indeed odd—*not* about my inability to pay. He might, he said, work out a fee adjustment. I could pay in installments. The work needed to be done.

If I wasn't attractive when I first walked into his office, I grew less so. How pretty can you be, walking around for a week at a time with your teeth encased in Peri-Pak, the periodontal equivalent of Silly Putty? To the casual observer, especially after lunch, it must have looked as though I had left the better part of a tuna-fish sandwich parked between my teeth.

At each appointment, the long needle of Novocaine penetrated my gums cleanly and swiftly. I never felt more than a pinprick and the pressure of his hand against my jaw. Things were moving along like clockwork. But one afternoon, he must have gone light on the anesthetic. I felt, suddenly, the sting of my flesh, hot and deep. My eyes squeezed shut; tears eked out of the corners. Dr. Ventura seemed flustered, disturbed. My evident discomfort made him nervous. Or else, he really shouldn't listen to *Carmen* while wielding a surgical instrument, at least not during the stirring refrain of the "Toreador Song." Anyway, he sliced into my lip.

It hadn't occurred to me that having an Italian dentist would be life-threatening, but that was before I'd driven in a car with him. Edward's car is a mini-opera house, and Edward is the featured tenor, singing along at top volume, arms waving. He's a passionate driver, to say the least. People steer clear of him—more, I suspect, because of the singing than the driving. It's truly painful to listen. Edward's favorite quote, not surprisingly, is from *The Importance of Being Earnest*, when Algernon says, "Anyone can sing in tune; I sing with wonderful feeling."

Trying to be cavalier, I asked him how many stitches he thought my lip would take.

"Oh, I don't know," he said, going along with my little joke. "Ever hem a skirt?"

I knew it wasn't much of a cut; but he was upset. Possibly he saw litigation leaping out of the chair and running down to the lawyer's office. I don't know. But that night, after profuse apologies, he called me to see how I was doing. I heard something in the background, a loud hum. He said it was his aquarium. I had to smile. Now this was more like it, more normal for a dentist. So we talked about his tropical fish. I didn't think much about that conversation at the time. Dr. Ventura was a nice man, so genuinely nice, it seemed, that it was just barely possible that dentists had gotten a lot of bad press. I didn't mind finding out if it was justified.

Dickens, whose judgments I trust in these matters, regards Edward warmly, but with some remove. He sits directly in front of Edward, a few feet away—close enough to be cordial, but a hair too far away to be touched. As you can see, Dickens and I are taking developments a day at a time.

To My Ex-Husband

MAY 25

This is so confusing that I don't know where to start.
It's taking me a while to get the full implications of all
you said yesterday when you came by. Just the fact of
your coming here was in itself surprising. Mostly—
nearly all—of our conversations are strictly business,
even when they concern Annie and Peter. Who's paying
for air fare home, who's paying for books, etc.

It was unnerving to have you sitting next to me in
the backyard, with the landscape of our marriage looking on, the same rooftops, the same trees, the same
rhododendrons, bending their leaves like so many eager
ears. I guess I was too stunned to respond. I'm sorry.

You say you're jealous about "this new thing" I'm
having. What was different about David? I remember
asking you then if you were at all jealous about that.
Don't you remember what you said? I sure do. You
said, "I would be jealous—if I felt about you the same
way I felt about Esther."

I suppose I asked for that. I thought, wrongly, that
I was hardened against any further pain and humiliation,
hardened against holding out any hope. That night, I
was in a horrible, nasty mood. David and I went to
see *The Purple Rose of Cairo*. I couldn't concentrate on
anything except his hand moving automatically back
and forth from his popcorn to his mouth, almost as if
he were in a trance. He seemed suddenly, excruciatingly
boring and boorish. When he was finished, he licked his
fingers, and put his arm around me. And then, with a

smack of the lips, he called me "hon." I hated being called that. It's a generic term of endearment, something you get from the woman who washes your hair in a beauty salon. It's easy and lazy. And it's not even a whole term of endearment; it's a half–term of endearment.

The truth is, you had rejected me, and now I did the only available thing, which was to turn around and reject him.

And now here you are, telling me that this is painful for you. Is it because you and Isabel aren't seeing each other anymore? Is it because you sense something potentially serious about Edward and me, and that it has occurred to you finally that leaving me might actually have long-term consequences?

But you were so magnanimous when we were separating. I was smart and attractive, you said, and had so much to offer, whereas you were middle-aged with no money and a family history of heart disease. (*Heart disease?* It was almost laughable, how you threw that in. That was the first I'd heard of it.) Anyway, I was a bargain—but not for you, who were old and poor and had every right, genetically speaking, to drop dead. It was better than a note from your doctor.

I have remembered all this, Nick, not just because of how shamefully duplicitous it looked when I found out about Esther, but because of how completely content you were with the notion that I might one day float off into another life with someone else. That may prove to be the one aspect that I can't forgive. That I could go, with your blessing. You wanted me to be happy. I was to understand that.

To My Ex-Husband

How I envy your freedom to conduct your social life in private. I enjoy having Peter and Annie around. Their presence confirms my image of myself as a parent, an image that suffers under the yoke of a single's life. So I'm most at home with myself when they're here; it feels natural. But there's this other problem. My dating life is monitored, every nuance taken in.

I don't think that Annie and Peter really care what I do so long as I don't embarrass them, or worse, involve them. They've been disappointed, disgusted. What are these supposed grown-ups *doing*, they must wonder. They'd like not to be involved. But they can't help observing—and absorbing—while resisting. It's as though they're watching a horror movie with their hand over their eyes and are helplessly compelled, peeking through their fingers.

This isn't me, I want to say. Only it *is* me, it's just not the me they know. And why should they, why should they want to? It's important for them to see the whole, not just the mother. But how painful and annoying that other part of mother must be when it serves merely to remind them of how their lives are changed, and, worse, that they're innocent and unwilling participants in that change.

It would help, as Nina reminds me, if you and I were to wind up in permanent, happier places. But we're free-floating, without any obvious direction.

J U L Y 2

Forgive me, Nick, if I'm missing something. But this sudden backpedaling seems adolescent to me. The more interest I show in Edward, the more interest you show in me. Is this really a sense of loss, as you put it, or is it competition, possession? I'm not being facetious, or glib. I really want to know. Because I do not, cannot, trust this feeling in you.

A U G U S T 3 1

What do you mean, "How could you?" As though I'd committed murder. Of course, it was a rhetorical question; you didn't expect an answer. But because I think it raises important differences between us, I'm going to give you one anyway.

I won't dismiss it by saying it wasn't easy. Just to take a vacation with another man and place my feet next to him in the sand was something of an issue for me. But I had to decide, early on, what was going to be off-limits. Was I never going to the island again in my life? And if I was, where exactly? On what street would I agree to rent a house? How close to the village? In which market would I shop, on which beaches would I dare to step? So I drew in my first breath on getting off the boat, and said, "There." I'd done it. One bogeyman down.

I could not go so far as to stay in the same house

that we went to with Annie and Peter for most of their childhoods. It was much too big and rambling, for one thing; but those summers in that house were sacrosanct. The rooms would have been full of ghosts, the children's noises, footsteps, even the way the water looked in the moonlight from the upstairs windows—so much I would not have had the energy to overcome.

You're forgetting, though, that not all our summers there were idyllic. I'm speaking particularly of the last one, in the cottage, when we were talking about the possibility of separating. "Where did it all go?" you asked me one night, holding your palms up to the ceiling.

I hate metaphysical ponderables like that. I guess I'm less heady than you are, too down-to-earth, and what I wanted to know was, simply, why you didn't love me anymore. You couldn't make love to me, couldn't pretend, even, couldn't get close enough for tenderness, for consolation. I was as lonely then as a woman could be, there with my non-husband, my non-lover.

Mostly what I remember about that time was lying in bed at night, trying to stifle the crying so that you wouldn't hear me in the next room. I'd emerge in the morning with bulging eyes and the thick upper lids of a frog. Yet no one who didn't know us would have guessed, as we walked along the road with Dickens, our arms wound tightly around each other, that we were a couple in the process of breaking up. No one would have guessed that the man who was leaning close to the woman at his side, pressing his head against hers, was asking as gently as he knew how whether there was anything he could do to make this easier for her.

One afternoon, being slow to wean myself of wifely duties, I cut your hair on the porch steps. I was cutting around your ear, and saw in your glasses the reflection of the daisies in the meadow behind me, across the road. And while I snipped, I considered that small framed bit of wildness that so typified what had been our paradise, and knew that a time would come when we would look back on this, on all we had, and wonder what the hell we thought we were doing.

I couldn't stand it. I wanted to pass away during the night, to magically stop breathing, so that I wouldn't have to wake up with that sickness rising in the pit of my stomach, remembering, as the early-morning light sifted into the room, that it was over.

I wanted to go home, I wanted to stay, I wanted to do anything to ease that pain, but I didn't have any idea what. So now you ask, how could I?

I could because I had a bitter taste about the place that had tainted my memories. But it wasn't the place that was wrong; it was you. You and me. So now I've done something about the place; I've given it a more positive slant. I couldn't, after all, do anything about you.

I said there were differences between us. I don't happen to share your impulse to remove everything from sight that could serve as a reminder of you, or of us. If I did, nearly everything around me would have to go. Then, when I'd gotten rid of all the things, I'd have to do something about the smells, the light at certain seasons of the year, certain cloud formations, music.

Imagine the music I could no longer listen to! You're in my blood, Nick. Don't you see? To protect myself from reminders, I'd have to close off my ears and my eyes, my every sense. I'd have to die.

I chose instead to live with it all, and thus live not only with it, but through it. I'm just starting to come out whole to the other side. This experience, this story, every detail of it, is part of me. I roll along, gathering myself toward completion. It's a growing process I don't ever expect to finish; but having survived each day, I wouldn't dream of lopping any of it off. I don't want to surround myself with a lot of unhappy memories any more than you do. But if I don't look them squarely in the face, if I don't accept them and take them in, who am I? I'm somebody who spends her life looking the other way.

I have to say that there were preoccupations with this vacation other than those presented by the past. More than being haunted by you and Annie and Peter, I was concerned about how to handle being with someone I didn't actually know that well on a twenty-four-hour basis. Edward and I had spent only one whole night together. Yes, we had made love several times, but only after three or four months of seeing each other. Even then, we were being chaperoned by Nina and Stephen at their house on Long Beach Island.

Nina was in her bedroom that Sunday morning—*the morning after*—and I ran in and leapt gleefully onto the bed like a kid who's high on cake. I thought I might be in love, and that if I were very careful not to say so out loud, it wouldn't go away. But I was so disgustingly radiant that I didn't have to say anything. She laughed and gave me the biggest hug, and I remember thinking how lucky I was to have a friend who could be so happy for me.

But until then it had been a rather cautious, old-fashioned sort of courtship. Edward and I would lie in bed together for hours and hours, making out and talking. It was like the '50's, except in those days we didn't say much. We just ground our bodies together until the guys complained of "seminal backup" and we girls whined about whisker-burn.

At first I wondered whether Edward was attracted to me, he was so unpushy. But then I got this picture of a man who'd been divorced for several years, and who had plenty of opportunity to recover. (He did a lot of "recovering," I gather.) I also realized without discussing it that he felt, as I did, that there was something to be said for being friends first. And yet I was intensely curious about him. I wanted to know what he would be like, the way he would breathe, the expression on his face, the force of his body against mine.

By the beginning of August, we had worked ourselves into such a pitch that we'd slip out of our houses on two or three hours' sleep and meet in the woods. Sometimes I'd bring a book that I wanted him to know about. I felt that to understand me he'd have to have read certain essays. So we'd walk, and I'd be reading aloud to him from *Private Lives in the Imperial City*. As the twigs snapped under our feet and Dickens sloshed through the creek, I'd rush through all the best essays, desperate to fill his mind with the same words, the same frames of reference, as mine. I never thought of it as foreplay, but that's what it was. It couldn't simply have been that I wanted to change my image of dentists as people who never read anything other than the copies of *People* that lie splashed across the coffee tables in their waiting rooms.

I adored the frenzy of that time. We were out of control, like two adolescents. And then, not long after, there we were, on vacation, having a sleep-over.

My first thought was that I wouldn't be able to go to the bathroom for two weeks. I'd be like those guys you told me about in basic training who couldn't "go" in a foxhole and were sent home, on the verge of being poisoned by their own waste. I would be carried by helicopter to the mainland, whisked along on a gurney, with this great distended belly, through the throngs of travelers in Logan Airport, to the waiting ambulance.

Fortunately, Edward was very discreet. Or else he reset his body clock for three A.M. In any case, our paths never crossed at crucial moments.

Thus the small hurdles of getting acquainted were overcome early on. The first night when we got into bed, Edward peeled off my nightgown and reached down to caress me. Just as I was getting aroused, he stopped suddenly, as if he had discovered that I'd shaved all my pubic hair off or something. Then he brought his hand out from under the sheet.

"What's this?" he asked, holding up the remains of a Monistat suppository that had failed to melt. It was the third night of a three-part treatment; treatments that are like second nature to me at this point. I had inserted it earlier, without thinking, and then forgotten about it.

"Well?" he said. I had taken one glance at the slender white worm that had become but a sliver of its former self and dived under the sheet. Edward was beside himself, gleefully insisting that I had, in a spasm of unadulterated pleasure, ejected it like a bullet.

Thus was the ice broken. By the next night, I was even able to brush my teeth beneath the critical eye of the professional. My flossing habits are less than systematic, but then Edward himself is nothing if not systematic in all things. He's the sort of person who always has his pencils sharpened, and a completed shopping list that he follows to the letter. He's not like me, someone who writes "trash bags" on her list, only to come home with a large roasting chicken. So there you are. The givens are understood. We're operating from different sides of the brain.

It might interest you to know that I am being schooled in opera—not that I'm a good student. I've told you that Edward adores opera; it's part of his genes, like the way he *knows* olive oil. He'll be in a restaurant, eating tuna carpaccio and suddenly, woefully, he'll shake his head. I don't ask anymore; I know what's wrong. It's the olive oil.

Even I, despite my reckless acceptance of almost any kind of food, have absorbed some of the finer points of olive oil. I've been less successful in the operatic milieu. Edward loves to test me; I, in turn, love to thwart him. Take *La Traviata*, for instance.

It's important to Edward that I understand not only the background of the story—that it's based on Dumas's play, *La Dame aux Caméllias*, et cetera—but the story itself, and which pieces of music go with which parts. I've always been content just to enjoy the music, while paying very little attention to what these people are actually saying. We'll be listening to the second act, and Edward will ask, "What's happening now?"

"Alfredo's father has just come to visit Violetta," I'll begin, promisingly. A small smile will appear on Edward's lips. I'll continue: "This is just after Alfredo has been singing about the idyllic happiness of his life with Violetta, rejoicing that she has so eagerly given up the excitement of Paris, where she had been such a social butterfly, to be with him in the seclusion of the country." So far so good. Edward is radiant. I have satisfied the true pedagogue in him.

"But," I go on, "Alfredo's father has come to say that she cannot remain with Alfredo because it is he who loves her, not his son. And anyway, Alfredo doesn't really love her; he loves Annina, Violetta's maid, and that, as a matter of fact, Annina is going to have Alfredo's baby." Edward has to laugh. But he wishes I would take my studies more seriously.

S E P T E M B E R   1 7

I guess you're angry. Having your estranged husband arrive at your front door and throw an overdue gas bill in your face is not a nice way to start the day. If Edward is in the habit of staying here when his children are with their mother, that's between him and me and has nothing to do with who should pay the gas bill. It always comes back to money, doesn't it? Like the roads that lead to Rome, everything boils down to what I owe you. Nothing's changed.

Do you remember having this exchange two years ago? I asked you not to come in the house anymore when you came to pick up Annie because I felt awkward, as if I were on display. You know what you said? "Then you pay the utilities."

Years ago, when separations were things that happened to other people, I remember some men being in a rage because the women they left were having people over to dinner—on the money that these men earned.

I never realized that the price of survival was so great. This vindictive, self-righteous stance is not like you, but then I'm sure that there are aspects of me, too, that strike you as startling. I'm more of a survivor than you thought, and more pragmatic. You might choose other words. "Hard," for instance. It's a choice of words men use when the women in their lives stop being accommodating and start doing something for themselves.

SEPTEMBER 26

Yesterday I saw Claire Edmonds coming out of Corelli's Market looking absolutely ashen. I was about to drive away, but she came over to the car and leaned in the window. "I just passed my ex-husband's pregnant wife on her way into the store," she said. Claire's such a private person, and we're not close. I've rarely seen her, except from a distance, since that night a couple of years ago, when all we suddenly single women had dinner at Isabel's. It was a measure of Claire's distress that she said anything to me.

She started to say something else, but dropped her head down onto her arm, which was resting in the window. Her shoulders were moving up and down, and I assumed she'd started crying. It must have been a full minute before I realized she was vomiting all down the side of the car.

What a strange experience, lifted out of the ordinariness of a day like that. I felt disoriented. In retrospect, my reaction struck me as strange, too, mechanical, almost as if I were not in the picture, but watching it. I got out of the car and went around to help, but I watched myself performing these motions—getting her a paper towel from Corelli's, wiping her face, noting, by the car door, that she seemed to have eaten a soft pretzel recently, all that—with total detachment.

Maybe Claire's position is too threatening for anything but detachment. I try to imagine what that would be like, to have to perform all the daily rituals of my life in the random presence of your second wife, radiant with child. In a few weeks, Claire will come face to face with the infant itself, a tiny blend of her former husband and her successor. Why does that fact, that there is a baby, make what happened between Claire and Rob so much more concrete, so much more real and awful? It's simple, I suppose. It's living, highly visible proof of a second union that, unlike the one before it, is fulfilling.

OCTOBER 9

It's hard for me to believe that I've agreed to this, especially considering that I feel, without giving it a name, that I've moved into some other phase of life. As I said, I'm distrustful of couples-counseling in the first place. And what am I supposed to say to Edward? He'll understand the reason for it, the need. And I believe he'll respect it. But that doesn't mean he's going to like it.

I'm not reneging on my promise. But this is more of a struggle for me than you seem to realize. Edward is not a diversion for me; it's far more substantial than that. You're asking me to hold all that in abeyance, now, and do this thing, this *process*, with you and Dr. Block.

I'm agreeing because I don't want to be someone who wouldn't. I don't want to be someone who would leave just because leaving is easier than dissecting a marriage and putting it back together. I don't want to look back someday and see myself as someone who discarded twenty years without trying to do otherwise. So, really, I'm doing this for me.

Still, I wonder: What's the game plan? What would we be working toward? Is this to find out why we're apart, or is it to see if there is any reason why we should be together?

You were unhappy, remember? That's why you left. Is it your plan to parade me in front of your doctor so that he can see what exactly is wrong with me and then help me/us fix it so that I'll be more acceptable to you?

But I'm already in the process of reconstruction, so that I can cohabit happily with myself. How do I reconcile what I'm doing for myself with what you'd like me to be doing with you and Dr. Block? Do I now walk into Dr. Bloom's office, and say, "Hold everything. We're going to make some adjustments in the blueprint. I thought I saw myself as a Victorian house with small, cozy parlors and a fireplace in every room, but scratch that. Nick needs me to be more of a loft"?

One other thing: In the last few months, you've seen quite a lot of Dr. Block. You've seen him twice a week, once in group therapy and once in individual therapy, and you say you've seen him for occasional "emergencies." In the last couple of months, you've seen more of Dr. Block than you saw of me during the last two years of our marriage. I feel that I'm at something of a disadvantage here. From where I sit, you two are thick as thieves. Dr. Block is *your guy*.

As I say, I'll go. But not without skepticism.

NOVEMBER 14

Sitting in Dr. Block's office yesterday, you said that for the first time you could see my "scars." How astounding that in 1986, more than two years after we separated, you would have your first glimpse of the pain I was in— have been in. So much of what we're doing now, this therapy, for instance, seems to be a delayed reaction. We should have been doing it two years ago, when you wouldn't consider it. These feelings you have—the wistfulness about our marriage, the agony of reliving our wedding day over and over, the loss of "my family," as you put it—make me want to scream at the top of my lungs, "Where have you been?"

If you didn't see any scars, it was, in part, because I hid them from you. I told you that while everyone else was reading books about *relationships*—yechh!—I was reading Miss Manners. She says that the smartest thing a dumped one can do is to get out of sight, or at least to hide all traces of misery. It isn't easy, but it takes the sufferer's mind off suffering so that he or she can start the recovery. It also makes one's former lover worry that this supposed act of cruelty was actually a relief to the one it was intended to hurt. And that hurts.

It was a game, and I don't like games. But I thought it was the only way I would get through it. I wanted you to be sorry. And now that you are, I can't say it feels good. When I see you cry, I feel the tears sliding down your face as if they were mine. I catch myself curling the back of my hand into my sleeve, and reaching up to my cheek to wipe them away.

On the way home, I feel guilty. *Look at what I'm doing to him*, I think. By the time I walk into the house I'm furious and I can't figure out why. I start slamming kitchen cabinets, and snapping at Dickens: "Finish your dinner!" And then I realize what I'm doing. I stop and ask what's this all about? Who am I angry with?

I'm angry with you for being miserable. Those damned tears—they make it seem like this thing was all my idea.

And then Edward calls, trying to get a reading on what's going on. He doesn't want specifics, he just wants to know: Where am I today? One of my friends—

I think it was June—said, when she first met Edward, that he seemed like someone who could be hurt. I passed that on to him. He said, "You tell June that I'm a big boy. I can take care of myself."

And he can. It's that confidence I find sexy. The man is no movie star. But there is simply no way I could convince him of that. He is so comfortable in his own skin, so sure of what he wants, that it's difficult to doubt him. He's my movie star; he's made it so.

Now all I have to do is figure out what I want; all I have to do is stop doubting myself.

N O V E M B E R   2 4

I know this won't be much consolation, but I do feel bad about Thanksgiving. But when you thought, Nick, that you wanted to think it over about coming to dinner, how long did you think I'd wait before making another plan? You seemed pretty sure that that would be too painful for you. I understood. Annie and Peter understood, or seem to have. The kids are long past the point when they expect us to do things together, ever. Frankly, I think it's easier for them if we don't.

It just hasn't been one of those easy, "amicable" arrangements that more civilized people have. It's up and down. Yes, we talk on the phone, and we've worked out who goes where for Christmas, and all that. We can do business. But we don't socialize. So maybe it was inappropriate of me to ask you to come for dinner in the first place. We'd been having so much more contact since seeing Dr. Block that it seemed like a natural enough thing. But, having taken your cue, I went ahead and invited Edward because his son and daughter will be with their mother and grandparents. Yes, it could be awkward. Anything—no, everything—I do is awkward. The kids think I'm playing musical boyfriends, and my mother, who says she likes Edward, insists on calling him Ethan.

1987

I don't know if I've given you an adequate picture of life here. The sleeping arrangements, for one thing, are not uncomplicated, especially during the holidays.

The Saturday after Christmas, in preparation for the arrival of Peter's girlfriend, I was performing what I understood to be an exercise in futility. I was making up the guest room. Washing sheets that would probably never come into contact with Sarah's skin, I had all the unsettling, if obvious, thoughts of a woman who knows that her role as a mother is more perfunctory than real. I was to look like a mother and talk like a mother while having all the personal interest of a proprietor of a bed and breakfast.

So, however I looked at it, I had my duties. I dusted the room, vacuumed up all the dust balls, put out clean towels, selecting those with the fewest number of strings hanging from the edges, made up a little basket of sweet-smelling soaps, and was finishing making the bed when Peter stepped into the room. "I think," he announced with a crooked little smile, "that if your boyfriend gets to sleep in your room, then my girlfriend should get to sleep in my room."

I dropped the pillows into their cases, spanked them hard in the centers, and plopped them into place like naughty children. As if to say, and that is that.

"This is Sarah's room for the time being," I said. "If she gets lost during the night, that's between you and her." The thing that's so stunning about this is not that kids are all doing it and being completely open about doing it, but that they're willing to have their parents involved. The very thought of having either of my parents within a six-mile radius of my sexual activity when I was their age was paralyzing.

When I was nineteen and spent the night at my boyfriend's house, my boyfriend's mother made me sleep on a cot placed, in a statement of trust, between her bed and the window. Now, I may have spent the entire night plotting my escape. I may have thought I would deftly slide over the edge of the bed, squeeze sideways through the three-inch space between the two mattresses, roll under her bed and fly, barefoot and breathless, down the hall. I may have been deterred, not by reasons of propriety, but by fear, wild and insane fear that maybe she had tied an invisible string to my wrist and to hers, and that I would turn the corner into my boyfriend's room to find that I had brought his mother with me. Or, typically insecure, maybe I was afraid that he was sound asleep and didn't really want me there. Whatever the reason, I was free of guilt in the morning, with no awkwardnesses, no regrets.

It's taken roughly twenty-three years for it to occur to me that those wakeful hours served a purpose, that in their own fashion they were well spent. I don't expect to convince Peter and Sarah of that. They're living in a different time, a time that is not going to spare them any trouble. Parents don't do what they used to do—regrettably. And so Peter and his friends are all going to have to grow up the hard, but possibly not the worst, way. They're going to have to do it by themselves.

You whispered, as we were leaving Dr. Block's office last time, that you thought I liked him. I do like him. He particularly endeared me to him when, at the start of our second session, he had clearly just been in the men's room. He had this little telltale water spot, about the size of a quarter on the front of his pants. It was a small window to his vulnerability, a great equalizer among men, and a tender reminder of you.

Your advocate, as I had feared he would be, hasn't pointed a long finger at me, saying in effect, "Well, no wonder. *Here's* Nick's problem."

I have this feeling, though, that he thinks this marriage is over, and more than that, he thinks it should be over, and he's trying to get you to see that. Why else would he mention, more than once, that the lifespan of the average marriage used to be about eleven years? So we would both be dead by now (or, at the very least, toothless), and rather than be consigned to a second lifetime with each other, we should do the sensible thing and get divorced.

What's he trying to get me to see? I don't know. Maybe he's daring me to think things I haven't dared to think. Not unlike Dr. Bloom.

I thought it was a telling omission, by the way, that he seemed never to have heard about Esther. But both you and Dr. Block wrote her off as though she were an insignificant character in an amateur theater production, somebody who walked onto stage left, delivered a dinner tray, bowed, and exited. I adore the notion, of course, that Esther has evolved into a sort of below-stairs person, as it were. But my God. To say now that you never loved her, or that you thought you loved her, but that "love" was the heading you gave it so that you could feel justified, like a job description . . . I don't know that I buy that.

FEBRUARY 9

We were at Cafe Nola when Nina told me that Esther was coming to town for a visit. It's a good thing I was eating; otherwise I would have been upset. Of course, I know Nina, and I know she did it deliberately. She was going to do a review for Wednesday's food section, and she figured that was the best way to break it to me, over shrimp remoulade and blackened redfish.

There's no reason why they shouldn't be friends. I just wish they weren't. Nina says that Esther and Don are building a house. I guess it's safer than having a baby.

FEBRUARY 24

My mother has a boyfriend. She's known him for forty-nine years, but now he's her boyfriend. I love it. Fred Graham and his wife, Lillian, came to our wedding, though you probably don't remember them. They were part of a group that used to get together to play canasta when I was growing up. When his wife died a little over a year ago, my mother went to the funeral and they got reacquainted. How could anyone have guessed then, as my parents, the Grahams, and the Wills sat around drinking their highballs, that one day there would be this big shake-up, and my mother would land in Fred Graham's lap?

The Grahams retired to Florida, to reenter our lives annually, on Christmas cards; Doug Will died, and his wife married her ex–brother-in-law and moved to Monterey.

This development on the part of my mother gives me a whole new, and not unprovocative, perspective on certain couples as I see them orbiting around the neighborhood on Saturdays. Maybe you're the one who'll live with Nina and retire to Wrinklewood. Stay tuned. Life can be pretty interesting after sixty-five, if you're around to participate. And if you're not, maybe there's satisfaction in the hereafter of knowing that you were one of the ones who made it all possible.

MARCH 6

Harvey had a date last weekend with a woman who's a really good friend of a really good friend of someone who works with Nina. I'd met her on a couple of occasions, and I thought she was terrific. So naturally we were all waiting to hear how it went. We didn't have to wait long. Harvey called me the next morning—from her place.

Not an unusual story in itself, but I found it disappointing because I know Harvey and I know what it means. It means that he has unwrapped the package and, knowing what is inside, he'll no longer be interested. Not, mind you, because there is anything wrong with the contents, but simply because he knows what they are.

Here we go again, I thought. And piles of packages to go before we sleep.

I have to remind myself that Harvey's just another guy. But, as you know, I've always felt so close to him that I believed we were practically the same person. All through our second adolescence, in our thirties, when we were smoking transcendental substances and staying up half the night to write "Saturday Night Live" skits that only we could have thought amusing—remember "The Turnpike Psychiatrist," who understood why you just *had* to pass?—having Harvey next to me was like having another me, only smarter and funnier and more disorganized. I was a watered-down version, and thus more conventional, but the essential person found in Harvey a twin. This aspect of him, though, the all-American guy part, this notch-in-the-belt stuff, is foreign to me, and I hate it.

As for *her* part, I don't know what to say. If Harvey's just into unwrapping packages, she might as well know it and be done with it. She's never been married, and has lived a quite exciting life on her own. Maybe she's used to it. Maybe she takes it in stride. Maybe she's a good sport. But it's such a waste. Harvey said he liked her—a lot. He said they had a great time. He confessed to me later, however, that she was "a little heavy." (Has Harvey looked at himself lately? If I had to choose between his body and his mind, I'd definitely take the mind.) So this is the story in a nutshell. Men are perfect, and women are grateful.

Meanwhile, June, who is all heat and no heart, and has always been the exception to any rule, has decided to exercise her libido by taking up with her mechanic, none other than the charming Klaus who declared our Beetle dead some years back. I can only conclude, despite telling me when we were in the car market, that the Mazda "vas a pice ov jonk," he had better luck with June's. Now *that*'s gratitude.

I wouldn't say this to just anyone, but I've always sort of lusted after Klaus myself, having a weakness for foreign accents. What stopped me were the fingertips. How does one proceed in any amorous fashion with insoluble wads of black grease stuck to one's fingers? But June's just marking time until she finds an investment banker, someone wholly unlike Harvey, someone steady and predictable, with zero creativity and unlimited funds.

A P R I L   2

Edward was waiting for me when I got home last night from our hour with Dr. Block. It wasn't the first time that he's been there to see the effect these sessions have, to take my temperature. I'm always a wreck. I don't want him to see how torn I am, because I know that would be hurtful; nor do I want to appear unmoved, which would be inaccurate.

I could tell by the way he walked over to the car that this time I would not have to find the right balance. The decision had been made for me.

I started to walk toward the house, but he stopped me. He wasn't coming inside. "I'm not asking you not to do this," he said. "I think you should do it. But I can't stand by and watch. And I can't promise I'll be here if you come back." And with that, he kissed me good-bye, told me he loved me, and left.

It was the right thing to do. Edward's not someone who would sit on the shelf. If he were, I wouldn't be interested in him. He's doing what he has to do; he's protecting himself.

My impulse was to run after him down the street. I had an image of catching up to him and begging him to roll down his windows, of his setting his jaw and driving faster and faster, more determined to shake me off.

I never had any illusions about Edward. He'll be all right, much more all right than I want to think about. But he isn't someone who pretends. This is hard for him, very hard.

And I have to be honest. I miss him. I can't listen to an opera. Last Sunday afternoon, public radio aired *Madama Butterfly*. I happened to tune in at the beginning of Act Two, when Butterfly is singing, *"Un bel di,"* which is about her joy on the day that Pinkerton's ship will sail into the harbor. My hand shot out to change the station, but the damage was done. For the rest of the day I was consumed with thoughts of Edward.

At the same time, I see you each week being more like the Nick I knew, affectionate, sensitive, and compassionate, the man who knew me, truly knew me, and cherished me. You did cherish me once. Nancy used to say that to me with such envy: *Nick cherishes you.* I believe you now; I believe *in* you. But even if you're sincere, is that good enough? Haven't we changed too much?

APRIL 29

I'm sorry to have upset you by calling you "Edward," though I'm not going to apologize for thinking of him, nor for wishing sometimes that I'd have a crisis, a hemorrhage of the gums, just so I might have an excuse to call him, though for professional reasons I've already been passed on to Edward's partner, a man who, I'm almost certain, gets his hair permed. Curettage will just never be the same.

Nina and Stephen saw Edward at Umbria having dinner recently with a woman who, by her description, sounds like someone he knew, a doctor, before he met me. "Phyllis the Physician," he used to call her. She's an internist, in which connection Edward has probably developed all kinds of mysterious and exotic malaises. Edward once told me he hated casual sex; Phyllis may have been an exception. He pointed her out to me once, some months ago, from a distance. She looked rather sultry, with full, flaccid lips. He told me that she liked whips and things, and liked to be tied up; I knew he was joking, but I couldn't get that impression out of my mind when I saw her, reading everything I had heard into a single glimpse. She was quite pretty, so I wanted to believe that she was a masochistic sort, given to severe periods of gloom and, most important, that he had never had any real interest in her.

Nina was no doubt hoping this piece of news would bring me to my senses. She's disgusted with me. She shouldn't be. She knows I've never had her clarity of thought, or her decisiveness. Besides which, women aren't supposed to be doing this anymore; mourning is something our mothers did. Today, we put everything behind us, wave it away. "He's history," we say.

She does like Edward; that makes it hard. And she likes him for me. To make matters worse, Edward's really fond of Nina and Stephen. He told me that if we broke up he'd continue to see them, that he had become their friend in his own right. We actually got into an argument about it, as though it had all gone sour and all that remained was to divide up the property. Over my dead body would he take another woman to Nina and Stephen's summer house, I said. He could see Stephen if he wanted to, though I'd prefer he didn't, but Nina was mine. So, for that matter, was Harvey, which was the next topic. Harvey happens to be yours, too, though, which is why Harvey's really the only person I can talk to about any of this. He carries the same sentimental baggage. He also knows you and shares my affection. I don't have to explain.

Part of my agenda with Nina yesterday at lunch was to go over some of the ground rules, a sort of friends-as-property agreement. We were supposed to meet at 1:15, which is in itself an imposition for someone like me, who's hungry by 10:30. She wanted to review a new Thai restaurant on Second Street. It was such a gorgeous day that I stood outside waiting. One always waits for Nina—and you thought *I* had no sense of time. At 1:35, I saw her hopping down the street. To her credit, she looked as though she were in a hurry, as though she did understand that she was late and that someone was waiting. But then she spotted some interesting items in a sidewalk display in front of a crafts store, and went in. I couldn't believe it. Nina is never too late to do a little shopping.

I ran down the street and practically dragged her out of the store by her hair. She wasn't even contrite. It was her way of exacting the price I would pay for seeing you. Nina does not want to hear about twenty-year investments, about the short term and long term. She doesn't want to hear about the Big Picture, at least not *our* Big Picture.

I sat across from her, with the steam from the *Tom Yum Goong* soup curling up into my nostrils, running out of adjectives. I said that if she didn't play fair, I would give away her identity; I would start some conspicuous note-taking. (Nina had ordered the *Thai Inter Duck* for herself, which made me a little cranky because that meant I would get a taste of that, while she would get a taste of the soup. What I wanted, since I outweigh Nina by about thirty pounds, and since it was hours past my lunch hour, was a taste of the soup and all but a bite of the duck. But there is, in this business, such a thing as a free lunch, and these were the rules.)

All the same, on a fuller stomach I might have more confidence in what you and I are doing, and more sensible resistance to Nina, who has her own agenda. Get rid of Nick; marry Edward. Period.

She's always said how much easier it is to leave a marriage and start over than it is to fix one. So many of our conversations revolve around whether people can really change. She's more doubtful than I.

MAY 10

I wanted to call you all day yesterday, but I didn't know what to say. Or maybe the problem was that I didn't know what to say first. I never went to sleep Saturday night, and I was pretty sure you hadn't, either. It was an awful night. Everything I said and did struck me as wrong and offensive. Everything you said and did struck me as vague and confusing.

There aren't many books on how to date one's estranged husband. Neither of us has been able to find the right note on how to behave.

First, the flowers. Opening the door and seeing you with the roses reminded me of that first anniversary after you left. You'd sent me a plant. I remember bursting into tears and being so undone that the delivery boy had to sign for me.

A single word didn't exist for what I felt at that moment; but the full reality of our positions came crashing down on me. I was touched that you had wanted to acknowledge the day in some way. At the same time, it was a sad reminder that on a day we once celebrated we were now living apart. Then, too, it was a public—by that I mean visible—gesture that should really have been private. Annie was naturally curious about where it had come from, and highly protective of you.

"Did you send him anything? No, of course not," she snapped before I could answer, and stormed out of the room. She had been seething in those days, but rarely had I been so aware of it as just then.

Anyway, it all came back on Saturday when I opened the door and saw you there with these roses and the sweetest smile. I wanted to be appreciative, but the flowers made me nervous. They seemed so bold, so red, so full of implication and expectation. There was even pressure in their perfume. Had I made a promise I couldn't keep? Worse, had I made one I couldn't remember? It was one statement to bring them, another to accept them. I was uncertain of both statements, uncertain and frightened.

And then dinner. The small talk of strangers tainted with the combined overtones of current enemies and former lovers. I didn't even know what I was eating, which has to be a first for me. I could only think one thing: *This isn't going to work.* Whatever happened, there would be that truth, and I didn't know if I could be the one to say it.

Later, when we were lying side by side in our old bed and letting the tears roll into our hairlines, I understood that the hard part had yet to come, and that was that we were going to have to let go at the same time. As long as one hangs on, it doesn't end. As long as one hangs on, there's guilt for the one who doesn't, which allows hope for the one who does.

I know you think I planned this. How often you've said, "I left, but you wanted me to leave." That isn't true, Nick. What's happened is that we've changed. It was you who said we wanted different things. I didn't see it clearly at the time. Especially since what you wanted at the time was Esther.

But, more and more, you like your life ordered. You make lists that you follow to the letter. They're little maps that take you through your day, your life. I notice how hard it is to fit me in, even for a discussion on what we're going to do for Peter's or Annie's birthday.

That walk we took a couple of weeks ago keeps running through my mind, over and over. I wanted to talk about us, anything that pertained to how we are, as people, suitable or unsuitable. I wanted to know how you felt about me. I wanted to know if you had *loved* Esther.

"Well, what's love?" you said.

Why is it that, up close, I never saw how elusive you could be? I didn't get answers, and so I must have made them up. You didn't speak for yourself. I spoke for you.

One thing you've said, and said consistently—that you didn't leave me for Esther, that you would have left me anyway. And yet you want to get back together. You say you've "murdered your family" and want it back. But I'm not the whole family; I'm part of it. The rest of the family is growing up. If we've done our job right, they'll stand poised on the edge of the nest, spread out their wings, and fly away.

When that happens, there will just be me, the one you were going to leave anyway. The one with whom you had dozens of long-standing grievances, the one who wasn't supportive or understanding, the one who made you feel inadequate, the one who left the financial realities to you while spending money we didn't have.

What makes you think I've kicked the Lord and Taylor habit? Don't you even want to check my credit rating first?

Lots of people reconcile to ease the pain. The problem is that they don't resolve anything. You said it yourself the other night. You said it so quietly and so quickly that the words almost evaporated before they brushed my ear. *I'm afraid that if we got back together, the same thing would happen all over again.*

And that's why we were crying, because we know that it would. I can't speak for you; but I've seen our marriage from a different perspective now. And that statement says it all. You keep telling me how much you love me, how much you want to be reconciled, and then almost as soon as I begin to move in your direction, you're filled with second thoughts. You *are* afraid. You're really not clear; you're riddled with doubt and ambivalence. You have little confidence in yourself and little confidence in us.

I might feel differently if you had more faith, if you had said, "We *won't* let the same thing happen again."

Like you, when I look at the span of our twenty years together, I tend to give it a romantic spin. That's why it's so tempting to step back in. I think of us working together in the garden, the way we used to; having long, intimate talks over coffee on Sunday mornings, the way we used to; exchanging casual caresses as we passed each other throughout the day, the way we used to.

I forget about moving to parallel positions, the way we used to, doing things side by side rather than together. I forget about the periods of feeling lonely, and the lack of passion. I forget about all the things we took for granted. I forget thinking that maybe we really weren't happy, the way we used to be.

So, *I* am not going to let the same thing happen all over again. This was easier when it was your decision. Now I'm bearing some of the burden. You broke my heart once, but you gave me an opportunity. And I'm sorry, Nick, but I am going to take it.

JUNE 3

Thanks for dropping off the material on divorce mediation, although "dropping off" doesn't exactly describe the way you flung it across the kitchen table, sending it crashing into the breakfast dishes. It's almost funny, a ready-made domestic cartoon. *I think we can handle this calmly, and in a civilized fashion, he said, throwing her down the elevator shaft.* Mediation just may not be for us.

Perhaps we could make a new sugar dish part of the property agreement. I understand that you're furious. You've been abandoned and all that; feelings I've never had, you understand. But can't we just get through this the best way we can?

JUNE 24

Well, you won't be hearing from a Mr. Mitchell Schein, in whose connection "nice divorce lawyer" may be a contradiction in terms. If people aren't out to screw each other when they start this process, the lawyers make sure that they are by the time they finish it. I see just how it must have been now for the Sands. They got remarried because they hated their lawyers so much. It was a hate that created a new and unbreakable bond.

Mr. Schein sat fingering a large, square diamond pinky ring while, speaking as quickly as I possibly could—you'd be surprised how quick, at $100/hr.—I told him what kind of person I thought you were, that initially you wanted the separation, but now I was the one who would be filing for divorce, that we were good friends, that we did not hate each other, that it was important to me to find a settlement that was fair. This was not just for my benefit, or for yours, but for Peter and Annie, whom I did not want involved in an ugly mess, watching their parents behave like vultures; that we had no money and very little property, only a house; that you were a painter and a teacher, and that I wanted to be sensitive to the limitations of your income while being realistic about mine.

He listened carefully, appreciatively, taking it all in. He had seemed a nice man, a family man. On the desk were pictures of him and his wife and children. One, taken of them all standing beside a swimming pool, included a big, yellow dog, like a golden retriever; another was of the three kids, two girls and a boy, on a sailboat.

When I had given Mr. Schein all the pertinent information, he let go of his ring and smiled. As he leaned over his desk, I couldn't help thinking that his face had a distorted, elongated look, as if reflected in a silver bowl. "He probably had some chippy, your husband," he said. That last bit, *your husband*, was spoken with a definitive nod, a punctuation mark that meant, "Come on, now. You can't be that naive. It's true, isn't it?"

I hadn't mentioned Esther. I didn't think he needed fodder. Furthermore, even I, in my admittedly biased opinion, do not harbor feelings of Esther as a "chippy"—especially since I think her parents named her after the heroine of the Book of Esther. In any case, your relationship with her should only have been that simple.

I have some other recommendations. One of them is a guy named Robert Seltzer. Isn't he the one who left his wife several years ago and married one of his clients, who was one of Peter's friend's mother? And then, after they bought this huge summer house on Long Beach Island, she sued him for divorce because she found out that he was having an affair with another client. I'm not absolutely sure, but I think that's the one. I don't think he'd take me on, though. I don't have enough assets.

J U L Y 7

My mother and her beau, who flew up for the weekend, were here for a grilled butterfly leg of lamb on the fourth. (I didn't want to compete with the sirloins of yore.) It was a little hard to get used to calling him "Fred." He was always Mr. Graham to me and my sister. I wish you could see him and my mother together; they're so *cute*. She's her usual quiet and unassuming self, but more relaxed than I've ever known her to be. And he, miraculously, wonderfully, is the same.

This is easy to say, in retrospect, but I always adored him, and if there were any other person I would have loved to have as my father, it would have been Fred. I loved his looseness, his gentle, teasing manner, his thick white hair, which must have turned light very prematurely. I can't remember it ever being any other color.

I never cared nearly as much for his wife. She seemed cold and cynical, particularly in contrast to Fred's warm gregariousness, and I wondered why he had married her, although there was never any evidence that they didn't get along.

I hadn't seen Fred since our wedding. I mean it when I say he's the same, except that the hugeness and the strength in the hug that enveloped me when I was a kid is diminished. It's odd that I didn't feel my father's absence at all. That whole part of their lives and all that went with it—my father, Lillian, the parties in pine-paneled recreation rooms, boating on Long Island

Sound, the canasta games—all had been peacefully packed away. They were playing a different game now. The music stopped, you ran for a chair, and did the best you could.

This time around, my mother got a chair. I hope she keeps it for a while.

JULY 30

I was bleaching my mustache when the doorbell rang. A crust of white creme was hardening on my upper lip. I'd just applied it, of course, and had six minutes to go. I'm accustomed to being caught in the midst of dealing with unwanted facial hair by untimely visits from meter readers and tireless idealists who make regular rounds on behalf of Greenpeace, and by the UPS driver, most recently a cheerful young woman who virtually hops from truck to door and back, having been liberated, I gather, from such female oppression as I was allowing myself to experience in midlife. But it was Edward's car that had pulled up in front of the house. He'd broken his resolve.

What a waste, I thought, running warm water into a washcloth. I had to wipe the stuff off. Edward would have been shocked, never having suspected me, I'm sure, of such deceitful practices. He might ask his daughter why, since she had such pretty cranberry hair, she dyed her roots brown. But daughters did those things. They tried blue hair, black hair, orange hair, spiked hair, uncombed, dirty, awful hair. They punctured their ears with a dozen holes. They dyed all their clothes black, or they pinned the legs of their jeans into a tight tube. It all depended. Daughters did that. They experimented.

But grown, emotionally secure women didn't fuss with themselves anymore. They were what they were; they worked with the givens. Edward did not like enhancements; I knew that. He was disappointed to learn, when we went away last summer, that I shaved under my arms. "I just want whatever it is that is you," he had said. "I want you that way."

There was such a thing, I decided, as being too literal. So here I was, touching up the shadows. But now they would have to wait. I would have to answer the door with a slightly pink, overly scrubbed face.

I hadn't spoken with Edward in weeks, not since before Nina mentioned to me that she'd seen him having dinner with Phyllis. I'd wanted to call him many times, fought calling him, but I was concerned about thinking in either/or terms. Just because it hadn't worked out with you didn't mean, necessarily, that it would work out with Edward. Maybe neither of you was appropriate for me. It wasn't just that I didn't want to be married to you; I didn't want to be married. I didn't know if I *could* be married, as accustomed as I am now to having things my way. I didn't know if I could make room for another person, another will. I'd lost my live-withability. For the present, I was like Candy in *The Cider House Rules.* I was waiting and seeing.

But the second I opened the door and let Edward in, it dawned on me that I probably wouldn't have to wait that long before I would see.

To My Ex-Husband

It *would* happen that in the week I'm supposed to be writing at a feverish pace about the "Key to Lasting Love," I have actually spent most of my time casting about for a lawyer to negotiate the terms of our divorce. I wanted someone that I could a) afford, and b) trust. What I found was someone who is part of a two-man office that looks like something out of an old private-eye movie, right down to the rippled glass door. There is a secretary, but she wasn't there, so Leon Fine was answering his own phone, which endeared him to me. I answer my own phone, too, so we were on an equal footing. He would be sensitive to my position without being what is known in the trade as a scumbag.

AUGUST 20

Life is good. I eat a lot of fresh vegetables, make love as often as I can, go to the theater at least once a week, and never use a vacuum cleaner. This in a note from our old friend Laney. Not a bad recipe for happiness for a single woman—for any woman. Especially the part about the vacuum cleaner.

I suppose it isn't accurate to think of myself as a single woman, since I've started doing so many things with Edward again. But I enjoy being able to choose whether I want to be alone or not. My Candy routine of waiting and seeing isn't exactly Edward's style, but he's okay about it. I suggested that his cooperation might have something to do with wanting to keep Phyllis the Physician in the wings, but he insisted that she was satisfactory only on a strictly emergency basis.

It's interesting that someone who was as riveted to the future as I was no longer has the need to know. I was practically born with that compulsion. Maybe that's why I threw away all my diaries before they had any value as history. It embarrassed me, even a week after any given entry, and in the privacy of my own room, to see how completely immersed I was in what was going to happen next. Every page began with a question, based more or less on a social issue. Of paramount importance, for instance, was whether Gordon Singer was going to ask me to the prom.

Not that I stopped asking such questions after I had the good sense to throw the thing away. I spared myself embarrassment of the written word by making my inquiries of a Magic 8 Ball. "Will I pass my algebra exam?" I asked, closing my eyes, all the better to concentrate on the powers that be. A cardboard triangle would float into view. Printed on its surface were the words, "Outlook Not So Good." Not being one to give up on reading the future, as opposed to studying, I then took the best-of-three approach. Two that said "Outlook Hopeful" would stack the deck, and I could go to bed. When other girls my age were wishing that they were prettier, or had bigger breasts, or that they would make the cheerleading squad, I was wishing for all that, too, but my biggest wish would have been that I were clairvoyant, that I could be my own crystal ball.

Of course, to see the future would be terrifying;

but what amazes me is that uncertainty is no longer frightening. I remember asking you before we were married whether you were going to protect me. I asked it in a half-mocking, coquettish sort of way, and you answered in the same way, but the words were right to the point. "There'll be good things that will happen to you, and bad things, and I'm not going to be able to do anything about them."

Those good things and bad things have happened, and what I have learned from them, without even realizing it, is that I'll be okay.

I just remembered something else you said around that time. "A good relationship is one in which nobody loses." I was trying to bludgeon you into going along with all my plans for the wedding without regard to the things that were important to you. I compromised for the wedding; you may have compromised too much in the marriage.

You told me one day, after we'd seen Dr. Block, that you made two mistakes. You said yes to Esther, and you left. Wrong.

You made only one mistake. You never conveyed to me how unhappy you were. You never conveyed to me the extent to which you thought you were losing.

SEPTEMBER 9

I'm always relieved when the kids are back at school, out of the line of fire. Every overheard word between you and me, each long, white envelope from Leon Fine's office that comes shooting through the mail slot is another step toward our divorce, another stone hurled in their direction, straight at the heart. But something happened when Edward and I were on Nantucket, and I was reminded that no one is ever safe.

The phone rang late at night. We'd gone into a deep sleep, after a big dinner and too much wine. It must have rung several times before Edward finally stumbled out of bed to answer it.

He managed a throaty, "Hello," and then he said nothing for the longest time. Whoever was calling had some serious talking to do. And then came these questions: "Who was drinking? . . . The police? . . . Which pillar? . . . You called Rescue? . . ."

I sat up in bed and hugged my knees. I had gathered by now that this was one of Edward's children, probably his son, Tony. I couldn't make out the rest of the conversation, which was muffled, but I could discern that it was conducted in the deep, stern, fatherly tones reserved for serious occasions.

When Edward came back to bed, he looked as if he'd plugged himself into an electric outlet. He'd been frantically running his fingers through his hair, a high-anxiety habit that I'd come to associate almost exclusively with his children.

"Here's the story," he said. "Tony had a party. Some kids were drinking beer, and standing around on the front porch. The music got pretty loud, and the police were summoned. In the meantime, one of the porch pillars fell down and hit a girl in the head. She seemed to be bleeding quite a lot, so Tony called Rescue. They took her to the emergency room, where she had a few stitches taken. But she's okay," he said, trying to calm himself. "She's okay; she's going to be okay."

Edward was not okay. And if he were within an arm's reach of Tony, Tony wouldn't be okay, either.

We didn't know what the police would do about the beer; the kids were all underage. We also didn't know what the girl's parents would do. "Okay" may not exactly sum up their impression of the evening.

Edward tried to get back to sleep, but it was hopeless. Every time he closed his eyes, the scene, and all its ramifications, grew larger and more terrifying.

The girl really was all right, and Edward hasn't heard from her parents. But there's no end to the horror that goes on in your mind, the things that might have happened that didn't—not this time. This time, we all escaped. But trouble is just around the corner, and kids do not understand that. Their complete lack of understanding, their almost willful ignorance of consequences, leaves them, and us, so vulnerable. We loathe them for their stupidity, while living in abject fear that they are going to do themselves in. They get older and they go away to school, and they get a little better at coping with reality. In time, they cease to be children. But we go on being their parents, wherever we are, and at any hour of the day or night, we can be struck down by that burden and by the limitlessness of its love.

Peter and Annie are ours forever. I used to think that as long as we were together, we could protect them, that we could keep them safe—a notion that is as absurd as it was once necessary to believe. The line of fire goes beyond us; it is infinite and eternal.

SEPTEMBER 19

Your lawyer is Sharon Glass? I can't believe it! You have chosen a "heavy-duty" divorce lawyer, by all accounts, a woman who happens to be married, not incidentally, to a man whose specialty is fixing noses. Marvin "Makeover" Glass, they call him. What a team. She wins her clients unconscionably large settlements, and he gets them all dolled up for recirculation in the meat market.

While I'm sitting in Leon Fine's office, explaining what a sweet, sensitive man you were—an *artist*, a man who could cry long before it was fashionable to do so—you're talking to Sharon Glass.

So much for sensitivity.

I'm as stunned by this as I would be to hear that you'd dropped your pants in public or pissed in the fountain at Logan Circle. It's as if you'd had a brain transplant and had become like that rich guy we used to know—I forget his name—who took a perverse pride in never reading a book and was in the habit of mooning in restaurants. He was thoroughly obnoxious and crass.

More than that, he was dumb. We were all dumb then, but he was king of the dumbs. Nick, what's happened to you?

It wasn't making any sense to me. Here was a man I'd loved very much, and all he wanted was a second chance. Going through these motions, asking for things to which I'd been assured I was entitled, bargaining on behalf of the rightness of my position—I just wasn't sure. I was acting on intuition, or worse, impulse. Would I regret what I was doing? Shouldn't it take more thought, more logic? Couldn't we just forget all this, I thought, and start over?

And then Leon Fine gets a letter from Sharon Glass. If I ever needed confirmation, that was it.

NOVEMBER 17

I wonder if kids have a pact. *Listen, if they ever break up, we don't talk to either of them about it, agreed?*

Annie called last night to tell me she thought she might have a ride home for Thanksgiving. Somehow, she got around to asking if we were going to sell the house. "I hope not," I said, "but it depends on what your father and I—"

Buzzwords: *your father and I.* "Never mind, Mom," she said. "I don't want to talk about it."

When my parents were getting divorced, it was they who didn't want to talk to us. "That's between your mother and me," my father would say. "It doesn't concern you."

I should have been so lucky that it didn't concern

me. Where I would be living, and with whom, where I'd be going to school. I was given to understand that it was self-centered to be curious about such things, so I learned not to ask; but I did offer an opinion once.

My parents had had an argument, a fight, really, the kind of fight in which suitcases start coming out of closets, drawers open, stockings and nightgowns are suddenly airborne across the room and into an American Tourister.

My mother was shrieking; my father put his arms around me, and I said, "The sooner you separate, the sooner you can get back together."

What was I talking about, I wonder—a fresh start? A virus that must be allowed to run its course? I don't know what I meant by it. In any case, my father agreed. "If only your mother could understand that," he said. But, of course, they never got back together.

What surprises me is that Annie and Peter don't even appear to be talking to each other about this. My sister and I talked plenty, although she had an it's-all-him philosophy that I never shared. I've always been more of the it-takes-two school of thought—until now, naturally, when I can see how the it's-all-him theory makes a certain amount of sense.

That's a joke, Nick. But I'm not going to help you out by noting, in writing, how I contributed to this situation.

DECEMBER 29

This seemed an empty week. The last-minute hysteria of Christmas is over, but there was something else: Dr. Bloom is no longer part of my calendar. I've terminated treatment, as they say. Only *he* never said that. He isn't one of *them*.

Psychiatrists are such a funny and varied lot—like the rest of the populace, of course, but more funny and more varied. Dr. Bloom seemed unusual in this regard. Normal, almost—just a regular guy, trained at a different job from the rest of us. Which is probably why I trusted him.

He wasn't going to be crass and vulgar just to get a reaction, like that marriage counselor we saw in the seventies. He wasn't going to be like the psychiatrist in my college town, who left his practice and his wife and children, to run off with a student and open a coffeehouse. He didn't have any bizarre nervous tics. Nor would he commit suicide, as Harvey's doctor had done years ago. Harvey's still angry about that. A doctor took all the riddles of his life to the grave with him, leaving Harvey to start all over again, which is probably why he hasn't gotten much done since then. He toys with his therapists now, charms them, as though he were at a cocktail party, collecting a few phone numbers, some more enhancements for his Rolodex. And why not?

I'd flirt with the mental-health establishment, too, if I thought the person I was paying two-fifty a minute to help me make sense of my life was going to close the door and shoot himself. Harvey jokes that he was the one who threw this man over the edge, that it was through Harvey that he recognized his own lack of insight. "I was too deep for him," he tells me. "I am, after all, a man of immense complexity."

We laugh, but Harvey may indeed be a man who can't be cured. That he doesn't want to be is another story. He doesn't want to give up his neuroses, he just wants to be more efficient with the ones he has. Anyway, I'm awfully glad he's my friend and not my patient.

No one, incidentally, has pronounced me cured. I can't remember how I came to be having my last session. Money was certainly an issue. But I also felt that were it not for the money, I would go on and on and on. I'd never run out of things to talk about, although the crisis that took me there had long passed. The things that upset me had less and less to do with me, and more to do with global events. Oil spills, politics. Sometimes we talked about movies. Dr. Bloom's slant, no matter what the subject, was always provocative and relevant. But then so was Nina's. She'd call me at eight-thirty in the morning, and say, "Did you read that article? Women should *not* be having babies after menopause. That's antisocial; it's rude!"

I had fallen out of love with Dr. Bloom, which was a good sign. How sad for psychiatrists, that their patients' ardor is just a phase in the treatment. I knew, in any case, that it was over when I started withholding things, editing my sessions, thinking, "Why, this is none of his business!" Of course, I still like him. I knew, though, that if we were to meet for lunch, say, even years from now, it would not be very interesting. It would be my turn to ask questions. I'd ask him about his wife and his children, and where he ever got that sport coat with the built-in belt. I'd ask him all the things that people ask of a stranger sitting next to them on a train, provided I were a chatty sort of traveler, which I'm not. Remove the intimacy of therapy and you're left with friendship. But there was no friendship.

Well, it didn't matter. We'd never have lunch. Dr. Bloom knew better than that. When I stood up at the end of my forty-five minutes, he shook my hand, and said something gracious about what a pleasure it had been to work with me. I noticed that he was wearing a nice suit; he'd improved his taste in clothes since I first started seeing him. And on my way to the parking lot, I wondered two things. First, whether he said that to all his patients, that they had been a pleasure to work with. And secondly, that suit—of a rich, deep-navy wool so soft it looked as if it had been woven around his body— had it been chosen that morning just for me?

1988

I thought, at first, that it was the beard. But really, it was what you said that got to me. *I'm never going to be that boy again.*

I don't know if I can fully explain what made me burst into tears. But I was shocked to open the door and see you, not reminiscent of the way you looked twenty-four years ago, but *exactly* the way you looked. You'd shaved it off so long ago that I'd forgotten. The face, the way we had loved each other when you had that face—it just didn't go with the anger. The anger is all you seem to have left for me. Think how you'd feel, Nick, if I showed up at your apartment, my hair in a shoulder-length flip, wearing an A-line skirt with that floral blouse from Peck & Peck, the one with the McMullen collar that I wore the night we met. These were the costumes of our courtship, the A-line skirt and the beard.

I was glad you had to get Peter off to the airport. I had to pull myself together, do all the ritualistic, motherly things a woman does when she says good-bye to her child, the hugs, the have-a-good-last-term. But I could hardly take my eyes off you. Watching you help Peter put his bags in the car, then lean down and pat Dickens—each gesture I took in as though absorbed in an old and cherished movie.

After you'd gone, I rolled it over and over: *I'm never going to be that boy again.* You say I don't acknowledge the changes you've made. Maybe that's true. It's true, too, that I liked the boy more than I liked the man. The boy had been so alive, so game. But the years went by and he became disillusioned. He didn't get the recognition he deserved. He "worked his balls off," as he put it, to maintain a standard of living that was insufficient. His family—his wife, particularly—was parasitic on his energies; demanding, needy. He got depressed. He lost the song he had. *I need new dreams*, he told his wife.

Yes, he made changes. But one critical change he does not seem to have made is in believing that his wife is the keeper of his dreams.

F E B R U A R Y   4

Settlement seems to be the topic of the day here in our town. Edward and I went for a bite to eat at Noodles and ran into Claire. She and her companion, a man I didn't recognize, were getting ready to leave. As she was buttoning up her coat, Claire came over to me and said, sotto voce, "Did you get the house? I got the house."

Rob was obviously feeling a little guiltier than you are.

I felt like a traitor to my sex, battling over percentages, in not asking for the whole pie. I *am* a traitor. I haven't learned to feel entitled. Entitlement is a male gene, whereas a woman seems to emerge undeserving from the womb and struggles her whole life to think otherwise. All I have to do is think of Annie, at two, sitting on the toilet. If Peter needed to pee, too, she simply moved back farther on the seat, to give him room. If he'd been sitting there, he'd have told her to wait. The whole toilet. The whole pie. Is there any difference? Entire books are written for people like me who don't know how to protect their interests. If I were someone who knew how to protect her interests, I wouldn't have married an artist in the first place. I wouldn't have been a writer. I'd have gone to law school and become one of those people who writes letters to me, "Re: Moore v. Moore." I would use phrases like "Affidavit of consent," and "stipulated value." I would promise to "effectuate the issuance" of my clients' divorce papers. But right now I am sitting in what has been referred to numerous times on stationery with engraved letter headings as "the marital home," and thinking that even one hundred percent of it for either of us would be the shabbiest victory.

MARCH 22

Slowly, the background is changing; a curtain is coming down on the old set. The props are small, though; it's not a major production. To begin with, I've changed my laundry detergent. No more Tide. My pillowcases smell like Solo, and by association, like Edward. Solo is Edward's soap. Solo in the laundry; Dove in the shower. Illicit scents brought into my house, scents of a man who is not my husband.

Habits get branded into your skin. Recently, I realized how infrequently I listened to music because so much of what I liked was linked to history. I hadn't avoided it; I just hadn't gone out of my way to sit down and pay attention to it. But yesterday, in the car, I tuned into public radio and heard an exquisite piece of music that I was sure I'd never heard before. When I got home, I called the station and was told that it was Jessye Norman singing Richard Strauss's *Vier Letze Lieder* ("Four Last Songs"). I went right out and bought the tape. You would love it. But now, of course, I've put my signature on it. Even if it's become a recent favorite, you will no longer let it in. "Four Last Songs" will not be for you.

Someone said to me not long ago, "Emily, you have a whole new life." But I do *not* have a new life. What I have is an eclectic, often uncomfortable, mixture of past and present. I have kept a lot of the old by choice. I thought it said something nice about me that I kept so much of my former life intact; it said I wasn't a person who threw things away. I wasn't a squanderer. I was sentimental; I had attachments. Some of that image, I see now, was an image I created for you. It made me more like you, and if I were like you, I'd be hard to reject. This for the same reason I took up yoga a few years ago. It was Eastern, intriguing, exotic. People who practiced yoga were intellectual.

If I were more intellectual, I thought, you wouldn't have left me. Not that you were ever pompous or superior. On the contrary, you were generous that way, you assumed that everybody was smart, even people who were clearly not. Anyway, you never talked in those terms. But it was a feeling I had that I hadn't been challenging enough. I hadn't been like Esther. Harvey was always telling me how smart he thought you were. Another word he used was "abstract."

Well, maybe if I concentrated on it, I could be smart and abstract, too. It would be like taking up occupancy in another brain. I'd shed the aspects of me that you'd rejected—the "controlling," "dependent," "childish" ones—and adapt new characteristics. I'd be completely different from the person who'd lost you.

Exotic, et cetera, cannot be grafted. In ten weeks, I went to my yoga class twice.

A P R I L   5

"It could happen to anyone," I said, "and does."
I'd stopped by to see June's new bachelor house. She was beside herself, sitting in her lovely sunny breakfast nook with a magnifying glass and a small plastic container. She'd show me the house in a minute; first, there was something more compelling she wanted to talk to me about.

For the last week, she'd been driven crazy by itching, an allergy, probably. To what, she couldn't say. She had no new soaps, no new underwear, no new nightgowns or sheets. But the itch persisted and kept her up at night. She called her doctor who, after persistent questioning, asked her whether she'd seen anything in her underwear, anything at all. No, she said, but . . . well, there were these tiny sandy-colored dots, pin-sized.

"Look carefully," the doctor said. "They probably move."

Move? A slowly dawning truth that turns the stomach: crabs. Of all people, June. So well-bred. So well-scrubbed. She had stopped seeing Klaus, as she knew she would, but not soon enough. He was apologetic, of course. Klaus is nothing if not gentlemanly—though an exception could certainly be made for this little incident. And he always did have a great sense of humor. That afternoon, he had delivered some flowers and a card. June showed me the card. On the front was a large penguin wearing a formal dinner jacket and carrying a silver tray of delectables. Inside, it said, "Just because you have crabs doesn't mean you're an expert on seafood."

Frankly, I thought it was hilarious. June did, too, although she refused to say so. "Look," she said, handing me the magnifying glass. "I've been picking them off. Even after using this medicated shampoo, some of them are still alive."

I peered into the dish. Like June, I was repelled but intensely curious. Sure enough, they were moving. Slowly and sideways, like real crabs. An undignified moment in an undignified stage of life. Somehow, we would all get through it.

I love talking to June now. She's so forthright, so earnest. I don't know anyone else who can talk about sex so openly, and without a trace of embarrassment.

I miss Harvey and June together. I miss the late nights and the talking and the big jugs of bad wine. I miss the occasions. They always rose to an occasion, playing off each other with an appreciation that never seemed false. They were a golden couple by night, two completely extraordinary people. By day they were just another couple who couldn't get along, who were willfully at odds. It was her silence pitted against his fury, his chaos and her secretiveness, his romanticism and her pragmatism, his fat and her hyperactivity, and finally, devastatingly, his blind adoration and her revulsion. As time goes by, it gets harder and harder to imagine that Harvey and June were once part of the same marriage, or, for that matter, that they could have participated in the same conversations. What sends a chill up my spine is that I know it's been said of us.

M A Y 3

It's awkward, having the same travel agent. So poor Shirley has a conflict of interest. You ask not to be seated next to me on the way out to Ann Arbor. I ask to be seated next to you. Whose request should be honored? Who's the troublemaker here? Is it the estranged wife who's only trying to be friends? Or is it the estranged husband who's only trying to be enemies?

My determination to be friends, to not let our divorce develop into a great continental divide, reminds me of my father during those hideous last months of my parents' marriage. My mother, who always maintained that silence was the ultimate weapon, had a habit of sulking, of drifting into a silent-movie routine, wordlessly placing his breakfast in front of him, including, on one occasion, an entire grapefruit, a big, yellow, uncut ball. My father always suspected that she stole that from Imogene Coca and Sid Caesar, but wouldn't have dared to bring it up.

For weeks at a time, the Woman Without Words, as my father called her, could not be reached for comment.

Finally, my father had decided he'd had enough. "All right," he said. "I've tried to be friends. If you don't want to be friends, the hell with you."

I may get to that point, too. In the meantime I'll just say that college graduations are just the beginning of many events in which we will appear as separate agents, rather than two people united in a journey that has brought something wonderful to fruition. Somehow, we're going to have to make that adjustment without ruining the occasion for our children. Sit next to someone else on the plane if you want to, but at the graduation be with me. That day is for Peter.

JUNE 10

We don't have sin anymore, you know. That has to be one of my all-time favorite lines, especially coming as it did from the lips of my mother. She's going to be living in the formerly sinful state, on the west coast of Florida, with Fred. She's sure that "tongues will wag" in the building where he lives, but she says this in the most mischievous way. She's thrilled with herself, and I'm thrilled for her.

I also wonder if our impending divorce has given her permission, whether until now she thought she needed to be a model for us of lifelong dedication to one partner. No matter that that partner was remarried, or even, that eventually, and in his own grand style, he died. The role of martyr wasn't exactly a struggle for her, as we know; she had a natural proclivity. That she's finally outgrown it has been her greatest gift to me. I'm sending her off with some new sheets and towels, just like a bride.

J U N E 2 8

Leon has forwarded a copy of your letter to me, written, I gather, under the direction of one Ms. Glass. You'll receive *our* response in a day or two, but I'd like to address one portion of your conditions directly, and that is the part that draws a cause-and-effect relationship between your continued payment of utilities and the possibility, in the future, of my "cohabiting with a man."

It strikes me, apart from its legal haughtiness, as a rather cozy phrase. I like its juicy intent. I hope you won't mind, then, if I pass it on to my mother, who in her renewed vigor will soon be doing same.

Am I to assume that if I cohabit with a woman, one, say, who pays rent, that you will continue to honor your commitment with respect to gas, et cetera? Surely you would concede that this would be no different from a man who pays rent, such as a student. Thus, the emphasis should not be on gender, but on the nature of the relationship. You want to make a distinction here between one who pays and one who doesn't, between an issue of money and one of affection, although it's my impression that the two are not necessarily mutually exclusive. And I could easily see to it that they weren't.

To My Ex-Husband

I wish, when you call to speak with Annie or Peter, you could bring yourself to extend to me the normal courtesies accorded the most casual acquaintances and complete strangers. "Let me speak to Peter," without so much as a "hello" is a real slap in the face. Which is why you do it. Which makes it worse.

Time, I keep telling myself, *time*. It's the only solution to so many problems. But it's not the answer someone like me wants to hear, someone who wants immediate and complete solutions to all things. Patience is a virtue; it isn't, regrettably, one of mine.

So, in time, you'll be less angry. In time, you'll accept that I care about you and love you, though I don't believe we'd be any more happily married now than we were before. I've been fond of reminding you these last couple of years that you were the one who was unhappy, that you were the one who left. I wasn't willing to accept then, let alone admit, my own unhappiness. In time, I hope you can forgive me for that.

Meanwhile, it's evident that you can hardly contain the rage you feel against me. It makes me feel guilty, knowing that it's borne of pain. I've survived, and you're having a bad time. So I bounce along after you, like a puppy, eager to make amends so you won't be angry. I want to protect you because you don't seem strong enough for the truth.

Recently, I read something in a book of quotes.

One that I thought particularly relevant, though I don't recall its author, was this:

> Real love is when you want the other person's good;
> Romantic love is when you want the other person.

When Esther and Don were able to work things out, I remember your asking me, didn't I want them to be happy. I couldn't bring myself to care about Esther's happiness at that point. I was more interested in Don's happiness, first because I always liked him a great deal, and second because he didn't have an affair with you. My point, though, is that you were rather magnanimous about Esther. You loved her. You wanted her good. How can I not draw the conclusion that you want less for me? You say you love me, but only if I stay married to you. Otherwise, you'd just as soon never see me again. As I've said before, that has more to do with power than with love.

A U G U S T   2 4

Edward moved in last weekend. I had been looking forward to living with him, but it was easy to look forward to living with Edward when all but the man himself was tucked safely away in another part of town. I had not considered his personal effects, which included his son and his daughter and their belongings, which, in turn, included some, but not all, of their friends and, in part, their friends' belongings.

The transition has not been smooth. But in terms of trauma, little could compare with the day itself, complicated by the fish. I did mention, didn't I, that Edward has fish? They live in fifty gallons of water, and moving arrangements can be unnerving. I pictured a major traffic tie-up as the fish slid off the dolly and out of their garbage can to flop around on the street, gasping for their beloved air stone. Nothing so dramatic as that happened, but two clown loaches were dead on arrival, or so Edward thought. They were only playing dead, though. They do that, on occasion. Hence, the name. Cute, huh?

It was tense getting them squared away. Edward tore around frantically with little nets and flexible tubes that looked like intravenous feeders. We had our own ICU. My concern was not that the fish would go belly up, but that the tank clashed with the couch. All that pastel paraphernalia—it's much too bright for an environment dominated by earth tones. I could see I would have to keep my aesthetic qualms to myself; Edward was dealing with life and death.

Both the fish and the children had to leave the home in which they were raised. Thus, the overriding atmosphere was one of resentment, relieved only by occasional moments of overt hostility, primarily on the part of Melissa, whose own telephone line had yet to be installed. Melissa is generally mute in my presence, unless speaking into a telephone. The phone is a social facilitator, the adolescent equivalent of a glass of wine. It has occurred to me, actually, that Melissa's voice may be activated by the phone, that words begin forming as the telephone comes within a range of perhaps three or four inches of her mouth. I'll have to watch more closely to see how this works.

Tony's grievance was mainly one of inconvenience. He was to leave for college in a few days, and this move meant an interim pain in the neck. It's stunning to see Peter's old room being converted into a gym; his old basketball hoop, still taped to the closet door, pales in comparison. Tony bench-presses. I knew this but, in a lapse of imagination, I hadn't seen in my mind's eye the equipment coming up the stairs, the duffle bags of sweats, the hundreds of weights—innocent-looking little disks until you bend over to pick one up and your fingertips get pinned to the floor. I guess he's not taking them with him on the plane.

By the end of the day, I was locked in the bathroom and crying into a gin and tonic, wondering, *What have I done?* It was like a bad dream in which you arrive at your front door only to find it altered to the point of being unrecognizable, a fun house, a horror of distorted images and mean laughter.

Everywhere there were piles of things that were not part of my life, children who had not been part of my life. We had no history together. How could I make them feel comfortable in a house that had been defined by the presence and the personalities of other children? How could I *comfort* them? I was not even their step-mother. Annie and Peter seemed suddenly to have been replaced. I wanted them back.

If this was difficult for me, it must have been torture for Melissa and Tony's mother, Pamela. What could a woman possibly feel when her children prefer to live with their father and a woman who is an almost total stranger? How could she possibly survive such a choice? It's like saying, "Mom, I can't be with you anymore. I love you, but Dad takes better care of me." Isn't that what it means? If you're a mother, you have failed at your job.

I've never met Pamela. I'd love to talk to her, but if I answer the phone when she calls to speak to Melissa, she hangs up.

Tony, meanwhile, has escaped to school on the west coast, where he spent exactly one day before buying a surf board and a wet suit.

SEPTEMBER 7

One of my first official acts as Edward's housemate was to pace back and forth at Jefferson Hospital last Friday morning, waiting for some young doctor to stem the tide of Edward's fathering potential. It should make a *vas deferens* in our sex life. Sorry; this experience has made me a little light-headed.

But if I'm light-headed, that doesn't begin to describe Edward. This is supposed to be a quick and simple procedure, "minor elective surgery." And yet, it seemed to be taking the longest time. I was getting nervous that they'd given him the wrong operation, that somebody had messed up the paperwork and he was having a lung removed.

My mind was alive with possibilities. It didn't help that I had read of a study in which monkeys fed a high-cholesterol diet showed that those that had also undergone vasectomies were more likely to develop clogged

arteries. Maybe the clog was actually sperm. It has to
go *somewhere*. Besides which, fettucini and cream were
staples in Edward's family. No doubt, had Edward been
a monkey, he would have suffered a heart attack years
ago, and the terror of a Novocaine needle would definitely have been a contributing factor.

I recall your being opposed to the surgery yourself
because you'd read all these nightmarish things about
what could go wrong. Women, of course, are used to
nightmares; they're doing things to their bodies all
the time. Diaphragms, hormones, intrauterine devices,
sponges, tubal ligations—always another thing to try.
But we did it; we did it all. It was our job. But men?
Well, what can I say? They're not so brave. Smarter,
maybe, not to endanger their health, but brave, no.

I was thinking about what I might say at the memo-
rial service when I spotted a man in a green surgical suit
wandering around as if he were looking for someone.
He spotted me, looking properly mournful.

"Are you Emily Moore?" he asked.

I nodded. This was it. Edward really had died. He
had not awakened from the anesthesia.

The doctor put his hand on my shoulder and bowed
his head. It was written all over his face, the shame.
This was the worst part about being a doctor, he was
thinking. Facing the family, the loved ones. Poor An-
thony and Melissa, semi-orphans. And Edward's father,
Mr. Ventura, seventy-one, widowed just a couple of
years ago, and now this.

"I don't know how to say this," the doctor said.
"Dr. Ventura passed out."

I thought, *Passed away, you mean.*

"He fainted just as we were giving him the Novocaine. He didn't want me to tell you, but I knew you'd be concerned. We got a late start because we had to be certain that he was stable before proceeding."

I was incredulous. My boyfriend, a wimp. I thought of all the times Edward had injected me with Novocaine during the days of my curettage, sometimes as many as four shots at one sitting. "This will sting a bit," he would say, dismissively. "But it's nothing, really." That phoney!

"Don't be too hard on him," the doctor cautioned sweetly as he walked away. "It happens all the time."

Edward was so thoroughly humiliated that it would actually have been more cruel than amusing to be hard on him. And, as a matter of fact, he restored himself in my esteem when, only a couple of hours later, he wanted to make love. He was tentative, naturally, but only because he felt funny without the full complement of his pubic hair. It was I who decided that we really should wait at least *one* day. I didn't want him to faint again, even in ecstacy.

What I did not realize at the time was that this procedure would turn Edward into something of a local hero. For the first hour that he was at home, he sat with his icepacks between his legs and talking on the phone with his friend, Rudy Nemerov. Rudy is Edward's Nina equivalent. They have always reminded me of Frog and Toad of *Frog and Toad Together*. Divorced at about the same time, they spent their early bachelorhoods giving dinner parties for all the women they knew in the neighborhood. They didn't ever really date these women; they were just friends they rounded up for some good food. Rudy was the creative force behind all the menus; Edward went by the rules, so if something didn't taste right he could always go to the book and see what he did wrong. It drives me crazy sometimes, and it drove Rudy crazy, too. But I figure it's an occupational hazard. I mean, you don't mix a little of this with a little of that in dentistry. You don't say to your patient when it doesn't work out, "Next time, maybe I'll put in more of the cement."

Anyway, Edward had to talk about his vasectomy the way women discuss their babies' deliveries. Rudy was fascinated, first and foremost by the fact that Edward had fainted. I could tell that Edward was sorry that he told him, but he never keeps anything from Rudy. It would be like lying to himself.

Rudy said he had never actually been able to go through with a vasectomy. He had too many friends who had problems. One of them had undergone *two* vasectomies. He had his seminal fluid tested after the first one, and the sperm were still swimming around. Rudy's friend was convinced that it hadn't worked because his surgeon was Catholic, and didn't believe in what he was doing. Another friend developed a huge mass on his testicles. I forget what that was all about, probably because Edward insisted on repeating this conversation to me at dinner and running the risk of ruining my appetite for grilled swordfish marinated in sesame oil and tamari.

I wish Melissa had been at home that night. She would have done me the favor of stopping Edward in mid-sentence by yelling, "Oh, gross!" and running to her room. And don't think Melissa's presence would have deterred him from discussing it. Ever the scientist, there is no subject that is off-limits to Edward, even with his children. I couldn't wait to tell Melissa that her father fainted, lest she think him impervious to the weaknesses of mortal men.

SEPTEMBER 26

Peter was sweet to try to break it gently to his grandmother that he and Sarah were living together, but that they *really did* plan to get married one day. My mother was actually funny about it, apparently. "Peter," she said, in that earnest, crackly little voice, "I hope you don't expect *me* to get married one day." Three generations all living in sin. Oh, that's right, I forgot. We don't have sin anymore. What could anybody say, anyway? It's really something when your grandmother is so outrageous that she paves the way for you. Next thing you know, she'll be backpacking her way up here from Florida on a moped.

One thing that Peter might not understand that the rest of us do is that not being married doesn't protect you from the pain if it doesn't work out. There is no shield from the ravages of love. There is only the strength to pick up the pieces.

Quite apart from love, there is something always to be said for pooling your resources. Annie certainly had mixed feelings about Edward's moving in and giving her room over to Melissa, although overall she's thought of it as kind of fun, like "The Brady Bunch." But you'd never believe how coldly practical she is.

When I told her that Edward and his ex-wife were putting their house on the market, and that it was time to make a decision about whether he and I would live together, she said, "Do it, Mom. He has a *much* better television, a VCR, and a KitchenAid. It's a good deal." Where did we get this kid?

She reminded me of your mother talking about the men in her retirement community. The ultimate qualification for eligibility was owning a car. He didn't necessarily have to be ambulatory. If you saw him actually move while sitting on a park bench, that made him an okay kind of guy.

If nothing else, I seem to have taught my daughter some survival techniques. A working dishwasher (with a brand name, yet) isn't the worst way to begin a new life.

Annie should only know what went through my mind when Edward and I were on vacation. Perhaps it was only cold feet, but I felt suddenly horribly trapped. Our days of being alone together were about to end. Melissa had decided not to divide her time any longer between Edward and her mother, which was certainly easy to understand. It isn't just that they don't get along; it's a jarring system. Joint custody is a fine notion, but the reality is unsettling at best, and the kids do all the adjusting. I remember Annie's saying to me, when all of her friends were packing up every other week and shuffling off to their other parent's house, that that was the one thing she refused to do.

I had always assumed that Edward and I would at least have alternate weeks to ourselves. But much of my anxiety had nothing to do with Melissa. It had to do with the loss of autonomy. I really had gotten used to doing things my own way, whether it was the order in which I ran errands on Saturdays or packing the car for a trip. There was no order; that was my order. A prerequisite of my life was that nothing could be planned. And if I blew it and lost out, that would be my problem. There wouldn't be anyone saying, "You see? Now look."

After you left, I did look, and I rather liked what happened. I had fun making my own mistakes. No one likes to be alone all the time, but after I met Edward, I had the choice. I could be alone or I could be with him. Now I would be with him. So who was sitting on the beach in August with her head in her hands and saying, "You see? Now look." *I* was.

OCTOBER 21

It's the first thing everybody thinks of when this happens, that it must be a car crash or a gas explosion. The house shakes, the dog runs under the bed, and you wake up and call the gas company. Hundreds of people do it. But not us. Not this time. This time, we were smart. We knew it was an earthquake.

Wrong. It was a crash, and it was a car. But it didn't hit another car. It came through the yard at 1:47 in the morning, demolished the gate and a portion of the fence, uprooted several shrubs, and sliced a sizeable chunk out of the dogwood tree.

And then it backed up, leaving a thick, black cloud of exhaust, and took off. Edward and I got to the front door just in time to see the left rear fender of Pamela's car going around the corner. But of course we can't be absolutely certain, although how many bright-yellow vintage Beetles do you see? Pamela the ex-wife. Pamela the alleged vandal.

Why did I have the feeling that she had gone around the block and was now parked in the dark, watching as we climbed over the debris, open-mouthed and stunned, in our night clothes? Surely, you wouldn't take that kind of risk without wanting to see the reaction. Such a violent and dramatic act deserved an audience. What an incredible letdown it would be just to go back to your apartment and go to bed.

If it was Pamela, how can I sleep comfortably in this house? How can I come and go, or let Annie and Peter stay here when they're at home, if the ex-wife of the man I live with is crazed? And what about Pamela's own children? They'd be in danger, too. They're traitors, after all. I have to believe that if it was Pamela, this is an isolated incident, an aberration. Still: I wait for the other shoe to drop. I go to bed at night and think, today she uses a car; what will it be tomorrow, a gun? Will she move from property to people?

Pamela has become an idea, a demon that runs rampant in my mind, simply by being an unknown quantity. I want to have lunch with her; I want to talk. The children of a woman I've never met move into my house and change my life. I want to give her a face.

If I could talk to Pamela, I could judge for myself. I'd know whether to be frightened or not. I'd know whether to worry that one morning Edward and the kids and I will be front-page news: DENTAL HYGIENIST

SETS FIRE TO HOUSE OF EX-HUSBAND, LOVER. It's scary, isn't it, that one day you fall in love with this petite and rather elegant woman who happens to be your assistant. And then, on another day, this very woman, the one you adored, decides that you're the enemy. She turns on you, wants to destroy you and everything connected with you.

I don't know any violent people; but if I had to think of someone capable of violence, it would most likely be a man. But I never expect violence from anybody. I think that's why I was so upset by the ending of *Shoot the Moon*. It wasn't out of character for that man, perhaps, but it was out of character for the men I knew. But I remember the anger building up, rolling to a pitch, like a summer storm. And then Albert Finney, as the estranged husband, taking his car and smashing the new tennis court and all its trappings to smithereens. Even he seems surprised by what he has done.

But women don't do this. Diane Keaton's lying in the bathtub and singing a Beatles' song—". . . But I couldn't stand the pain . . ."—struck me as a much truer chord. It was something I would do, something I have done.

As I said, I don't know Pamela, but this isn't the Pamela I've heard about, sweet, vulnerable. Angry, yes. But far more self-destructive than violent. I'm sure Tony and Melissa wouldn't believe she would be capable of doing anything like this, nor would Edward. But for having seen the yellow car that has given such fuel to my imagination, it would never occur to any of us that it was somebody we know.

Meanwhile, in my head I have this portrait of a

marriage between a healthy, level-headed man and a hysteric that may have no bearing on the truth. And if I think about what happened not as an act of violence, but one of passion, I see it differently. And I see anybody, anybody at all, passionately wanting to do something insane and satisfying. And why not do it to the one we think destroyed our life?

We live with a person for ten, fifteen, twenty, or thirty years. We know all that person's weaknesses and failures. What is it about that knowledge, being *known*, that eats away at us and turns to poison? It's because that knowledge reflects. Your spouse becomes a mirror, and the closer you get to him, the more you see yourself, and the more you hate what you see.

N O V E M B E R   3

Leon Fine called yesterday and said, "Congratulations!"

I thought he was being sarcastic. He knows I wouldn't have voted for George Bush. Then, because I didn't get it, he said, "Emily, you're a divorced woman."

It sounded all wrong to me. Congratulations are for things one can be proud of; I was anything but proud. The reality is emotionally devastating and shameful. I'm *ashamed*. Then, this afternoon, the papers came. There is this phrase, "Irretrievable breakdown," printed in the upper right hand corner of the decree. It sounds like a rude and incorrect diagnosis that belongs to some other couple. Is this really *us*?

We're just another statistic now, just another failure. But there's something else about the fact of the divorce that deeply disturbs me, something I hadn't adequately prepared myself for. I don't like the word "divorce" or the image it evokes, though there was a time when divorce—and divorcée—had a chic, Wallis Simpson ring to it. Now I'm appalled. It's just not how I see myself, as someone who gets divorced.

I like to think, as I guess everyone who goes through it does, that our divorce isn't *one of those*, that it's different. I continue to believe that I had the right instincts, married the right person. For two decades you were someone I looked forward to seeing every day. A woman once said to me, "If you are what you choose, you choose something different at forty than you do at twenty-five." It's true that I might not choose you today; but there is no question that I would, that I have in many respects, chosen the *kind* of man that you are. You're not reaching into a different drawer when you settle in with a second person. You're still looking for some level of integrity and sensitivity and humor. If we can't live together happily, that doesn't mean that you aren't still important to me as any man, any person, could be; you're the one who gave me my connection to the world.

I don't know if you remember my old high school friend Louise. She wrote me a letter recently that contained the usual catch-up data, the work she's doing as the new pastor of her church, news of her children, what their interests are. Then there was this paragraph that began, "John and I still manage to find each other exciting and interesting . . ."

With those words, I felt the enormity of the loss all

over again. I haven't been able to write back. I can't face our relative positions. Here's a woman who would never be separated, never be divorced. She always had such clarity, such personal strength, that that kind of failure would always be outside her.

Nor have I written to either my high school or my college alumnae office to tell them my newest news, that I have just received congratulations on my divorce, that the life I have led since my school days could be summed up in a single, tight-lipped exchange between confidantes: *Did you get the house? I got the house.*

Not that anyone would be surprised. Sometime on a visit home from college during my freshman year, I went back to my high school, and was talking with a former, and formidable, teacher. I was on academic probation at the time, an apparently unstartling development to this woman who met my announcement with an indifferent silence, borne, I believed, of abject boredom. To ease my discomfort, I quickly added, "But Louise is doing very well."

"Yes," she replied curtly, "one would have expected her to do well."

Now I imagine meeting that teacher once again, in just that way, standing awkwardly in the same hallowed hall and telling her of Louise's entrance into the ministry—and my divorce. "Yes," she would say, as though she already knew. "Of course."

Was it an illusion—tell me it wasn't—that we did some things effectively? Last spring, at Peter's graduation, as we were sitting out on that lush lawn and holding hands, waiting for him to walk across the stage and collect his degree, I thought that despite the upheaval and all its attendant misery, we had managed together to raise two very fine people; that there was a rightness in these events that is mercifully both reassuring and irrevocable. I also thought that there was no one else I would have wanted beside me but you.

NOVEMBER 17

It just ruins a meal to try to talk to Nina about you. She refuses to participate in the post-mortems. She says I'm boring on the subject, that I make her crazy. She makes a decision. Snap, snap. She doesn't look back, whereas I look back every day. I need to see where I've been. This is not to say that I live in the past, but that the past is the only way I can understand the present.

Somebody once told me (I have no idea who, but I guess we know it wasn't Nina) that there's a year of mourning for every three years of marriage. Her point was that we *must* go through the process. Otherwise, it'll catch up to us one day, possibly even years from now, and we'll be paralyzed by guilt and remorse. I don't know whose formula this is, but if it has any validity, we have a few years to go.

DECEMBER 1

I never thought that I would come to a point in my life in which there would be piles and piles of lovely, lacy bras in a rainbow of seductive colors emerging from the "delicate" cycle of my washing machine. If Whirlpools could talk! This is serious lingerie, with underwire supports and cups in a size that is a little farther along in the alphabet than I'm accustomed to. It's like living in a Victoria's Secret catalog.

Nick, there is a nymph in my house. Melissa looks like something out of *A Midsummer Night's Dream*, but, unfortunately, she has all the earthly qualities of the quintessential teenager. Just taking a shower is a trial. You can't get to the water without fighting your way through seventeen different kinds of shampoos and conditioners, disposable razors that never get disposed of, facial sponges, brushes, henna rinses, and the hair itself, which gathers, like a cough ball, on the screen over the drain. The nail supplies have been summarily removed (by me) and put back in her room. Soon it will be necessary to build an annex just to contain the beauty products.

I begin to see Pamela for what she is—smart. Really smart. Would that *I* could see Melissa every now and then and take her out to dinner. Every time her door slams or the volume goes up on her stereo, or six of her friends come home with her at two A.M. after a party, I think, Pamela must be laughing herself sick. How silly of me to think she'd be concerned about how I deal with her daughter, or how her daughter deals with me. All she's thinking is "Better her than me."

I enjoyed Annie and Peter's adolescence, although a universal exception could be made for thirteen-year-old girls. Nina and I were always calling each other on mornings that had gotten off to a bad start. Invariably the conversation would begin with, "Don't you just *hate* them?"

Melissa's seventeen, not thirteen, thank God. But Annie will be graduating in the spring. Had I arranged my life differently, I might have been free to take a deep breath and enjoy the solitude while sitting around waiting for the grandchildren to come. Instead, I'll be here, escalating the aging process. For sure, I'll be deaf in no time. (By the way, it wasn't Pamela who drove through the yard. Melissa happened to mention some time later that her mother was hiking in the Northwest with the Sierra Club at the time. Such a wholesome activity. I should bite my tongue.)

I wonder whether you worry about Dickens, how he fares as the pet of another man. The truth is, he's having a big sulk. It hasn't been easy for an old dog, all these changes. Tony has been his pal, but Tony won't be at home until Christmas. Edward is Dickens' pal, too, but his is an old-fashioned devotion, with a built-in this-hurts-me-more-than-it-hurts-you kind of discipline. This, as he removes Dickens' two front paws from the table, plopping him back down on all fours. Edward has what some people would call an "attitude" about dogs, which is that they are dogs.

As you and I know, this has never been Dickens' position. We were a democratic unit here, once upon a time. The law of the land seems grossly unjust these days; so much is done to ease the transition for Melissa, who parades around the house talking on her new portable telephone. She brings it to the dinner table, where it is placed squarely to the left of her plate, along with her fork. *We* would not have allowed this. I tell Edward that if he had the same standard of behavior for Melissa that he has for Dickens, life would be a lot more pleasant. If Dickens doesn't like what he gets for dinner, he has the option of rejecting it until he starves to death. "When he gets hungry, he'll eat it," says Edward. Melissa, on the other hand, is free to fix herself something else. And if she doesn't feel like it? Edward will fix it. So she doesn't starve to death.

DECEMBER 18

The holidays should be interesting. Melissa will be here; Tony will be here; Annie will be here, relegated to the guest room. Peter and Sarah are taking the week between Christmas and New Year's off, and are going to spend half of it here and half of it with her parents. Tony's agreed to sleep on the floor in Melissa's room during that time, unless he brings his new girlfriend, whose parents are going to be visiting her sister in Florence. In that case, maybe they could stay with the people who bought Edward's house. My mother and Fred are coming too, but I've got a hotel room for them. Now what I'd like to do is get one for myself.

All the Christmas rituals that have been tidily confined to individual households will be on a crash course under one roof. Annie will insist on the usual Moore Christmas tree, short and fat. Tony goes for the statuesque type that grazes the ceiling, something only slightly taller, say, than the one at Rockefeller Center. Melissa won't really care what kind of tree we get so long as there's plenty of stuff under it. Naturally, none of the kids will want to bother going with us to get the tree. They'll all put their vote in and then leave it to us to make it count. Edward and I will be scurrying around the Christmas-tree lot, hopping up and down trying to keep warm and arguing about how the compromise tree leans—too much toward the Moore ideal, or the Ventura ideal.

None of this takes into account, however, the inevitable balsam/Douglas fir controversy that is certain to arise, the lovely aroma of the former versus the needle staying power of the latter. Edward himself would go for something roughly two feet high and unscented, in acrylic.

Still to be settled is whether we do gifts on Christmas Eve, as they have always done, or on Christmas morning, as we have always done. If the Christmas Eve tradition prevails, Annie will have to open hers later, by herself. She'll be with you on Christmas Eve.

June told me that you've bought a house. She says it's completely charming, and has an extra bedroom. I don't suppose you'll be moving in time for Christmas . . .

1989

Another new year—and early menopause! I'm not a
Brady Bunch kind of woman, I can see that. I wonder
if there was an episode in which the mother didn't get
her period for months on end, a situation much exacer-
bated by the holidays.

Being at home does not bring out the best in children. In terms of behavior, I would set the average age
at about five. They play in their rooms with their respec-
tive friends until Edward and I announce that dinner is
ready, at which time they come skipping and squealing
into the kitchen, look at their food, pick it over, and say
"What's in it?" Then, as the meal progresses and Edward
and I ask that they try to refrain from sprawling across
the table, they whine. "It's not like it's a formal dinner
party, Dad."

If they were five, you could say, "Go to your
room." Only since most of them are in college, you'd
have to say, "Go to your guest room."

Tony's girlfriend was perfectly delightful, though,
and very solicitous of Annie, who felt left out. Edward
and I kept asking each other, "Now why couldn't our
children be like *that?*" Nina, in her usual sane voice,
has reminded me that our children *are* like that—when
they're at someone else's house.

Now we're whittled back down to just Melissa.
Edward describes life with Melissa as like in a "demil-
itarized zone." But Edward himself is no day at the
beach when she's at home. They're like a cat and dog
circling each other around the food bowl. It occurs to

me occasionally that Melissa is fine—that Edward is the problem.

In any event, we've made progress. Recently, Melissa asked me a direct question—her first. (This is someone, bear in mind, who calls her father at work to let him know that there's nothing in the refrigerator that she likes to eat. There's none of *her* food. Not that identifying her food is that simple. She no longer eats anything that's been tied up or has a face. She was eating yogurt, but now milk products are suspect. So we're pretty much down to pasta and free-range lettuce.) Anyway, Melissa wanted to know, was I going to let my hair get gray?

"To match my clothes?" I asked. She had used the washing machine to dye some shirts black, and the dye was still in the machine the next time I used it. With my gray clothes and my gray hair, I'd be an adolescent's dream. Put me against a gray January sky and I'd be invisible.

Melissa's question touched me in a funny way. It meant she had a view of what she wanted her father's girlfriend to be like, or at least to look like. That meant that she had an opinion. She wasn't indifferent, as I had thought. She didn't say it, but I assumed that she didn't want me to let my hair get gray, which presented something of a dilemma. *I* wanted to let my hair get gray. At the same time, I wanted to please Melissa. I wasn't indifferent, either. The girl is growing on me.

Melissa is in the habit of wearing big clothes, things that don't actually come in contact with her body. The clothes in combination with this full, wavy head of honey-colored hair give her a rag doll quality that perhaps

I'd begun to find irresistible. That, and the gnawing awareness of how hard it must be to be uprooted at that age, to give up your room, your house, your street, the path to your friend's house, your bus stop; to find yourself with a whole new set of territorial imperatives, to suffer the scrutiny of people who feel like aliens to you, people who want you to do things for-your-own-good, people who think they are interested in who you are, but who will not rest until you are more like them. I'd developed a need to pick Melissa up, sit her in my lap, and read her a story. But no story would be enough; it's never enough to say, I know how you feel.

FEBRUARY 6

There was a time (during our marriage, for instance) when a man was out of place in the kitchen. He was a vestigial organ that hung about with his hands in his pockets, asking if there was anything he could do. Cooking was a gene thing. To ask your husband to prepare dinner was as outrageous as asking him to change the color of his eyes. So I secretly longed for a man who would step into the kitchen, step up to the stove, and say, "Well, tonight we're having noisettes of lamb with a raspberry vinegar sauce."

Of course, it needn't have been anything so grand as all that. I would have been grateful with some cozy, competent middle ground between the Frugal Gourmet and you, the fellow who used to get me out of the shower because the rice had come to a boil.

I remember, some years ago, forming a prophetic

opinion about all this. Harvey was making an omelet that was a work of art. From the first flick of the wrist as he cracked the eggs to the final product as it flipped up into the air and came down in the pan, I felt as if he had donned a cape and flown out of a phone booth. It was then I decided that if I ever married again it would not be for money, nor even, necessarily, for love. It would be for that omelet, that sparkle of perfection that had danced in my dreams. I would commit myself forever to the first man who could make it.

This was, as we say today, in another life. Now, in my new life, I am putting the cover on a pot of peas. The sound of the lid clicking into place stirs a proprietary interest on the other side of the room. It is he who has passed the omelet test. "Just a minute," he says, rushing to the rescue. "Wait for the water to boil first. Then put the cover on."

"Does it really matter?" I ask, knowing it doesn't. I know, you see, because I have been cooking peas for a quarter-century. He can tell me about the *soufflé de saumon* if he wants to. He can tell me about the *champignons farcis*. But he cannot tell me about peas.

"Yes, it matters," he says. "Part of the cooking process is the gradual increase in heat . . ."

Okay, so he can tell me about peas. All the better to move on to the salad dressing, my area of expertise. I use my usual, time-honored recipe of lemon, olive oil, a touch of tarragon, and a bit of mustard. I like it, the children like it, my ex-husband—where are you when I need you?—always liked it.

Edward, however, does not like it. One dip of the finger determines that it "lacks zip." But not to worry.

What I have here, he explains gently, as if speaking to a small child, is not a salad dressing, but the basis for a salad dressing. He will add pepper and Parmesan, more mustard, maybe, and some garlic. What do I think?

What do I *think*? I think, Why don't I just go get a glass of wine and lie down?

What is this? Has my mother forgotten to tell me something? Why would a woman sit her daughter down and discuss the ways of the world and, more specifically, the ways of men, and neglect to mention the apparently incontrovertible importance of a gradual increase in heat? With respect to peas, I mean.

And that's not all. Recently, while I was performing that most familial of culinary tasks, baking a cake, Edward made a seemingly simple inquiry. Had I tested the baking powder to see if it was still good?

This may be naive on my part, but I take the shelf life of my baking powder for granted, not unlike that Fire 'n' Ice lipstick rolling around in my medicine cabinet that dates back to the fifties. Slices of roast beef, or pints of cream, they're something else. They scream to be released at a certain point. My mother must have felt that way, too. Otherwise, she surely would have clued me in about the all-important baking-powder test.

Frankly, it's more than I want to know. And, at the risk of being ungrateful, I feel similarly about the top on the pot of peas.

And so, in having surrendered sovereignty of the stove to a higher and, in this instance, masculine authority, I reflect: Maybe I never made mouths water; maybe I stunted the cultural growth of a trusting and innocent family by stooping to use the blender method for the béarnaise. Now, thanks to an answered prayer, the culinary equivalent of the Second Coming, I know better. But I'm reminded of an old expression that the enlightened often impart to the unenlightened: "You don't know what you're missing." It seems a glib and rather reckless statement. For it may not be the best thing to find out. To know can mean to fall from grace. You can be a second-class citizen in your own kitchen. Far wiser, then, to heed those who warn, "Be careful what it is you ask for. You might get it."

FEBRUARY 23

Nina's father died last week. He was buried, which surprised me. I didn't know him so well that I could really speculate on his wishes with any accuracy, but I didn't think he was a religious man. He never made a point of his religion, at least not publicly. Now, it turns out, he had converted to Catholicism in his later years. No one seemed aware of that, even Nina and her mother, except in the vaguest way, and it was their job to put together the suit, tie, and shoes that he was to wear for burial.

  None of this, of course, is unusual in itself. But it made me think of how we sign our name, so to speak, when we take our leave of this world. It's our final stamp, the mark of who we are. What I don't understand is why that mark is so often a secret, a posthumous message left in a sealed envelope under a blotter on the deceased's desk. My father went so far as to buy a burial plot—and then scribbled frantically at the eleventh hour that he wanted to be cremated.

Maybe it seemed like too much trouble, suddenly, that someone would have to go around shopping for a casket. Or maybe he was disturbed by the notion of being hermetically sealed, preserved in the earth, rather than being permitted to return to it. But it begins to make sense to me now about him, not what he wanted, but that he changed his mind about what he wanted. He was a man who switched signals. This was his final, signature switch.

I've always wanted to tell you what it was like at the crematory that morning, but there never seemed an appropriate time. You discouraged me from going; everybody did. The reason it wasn't discussed may have been out of deference to Annie and Peter, who would have been completely freaked out by the idea, or perhaps it had more to do with us. Our marriage was distinguished in those days more by what wasn't said than by what was.

I might have done it out of rebellion, but I'm glad I did. Someone comes and zips your father into a body bag and takes him away. It's the last you see of him. There's no viewing, no grave where you'll sit with a bunch of daisies and commune with the man who made you happy and miserable in equal measure for as long as you knew him.

So I had to see where they took him and what they did to him. I told the driver I'd follow; he didn't seem to mind. Though I knew better, I had a child's image of the place where we were headed: figures of hooded death standing on guard at the gates; thick, black smoke curling about the roof; bodies waiting for the iron jaws of the oven to clang shut on their last light of day. We pulled up in front of a one-story cinder-block building. For a second, I thought that the driver was making an unscheduled stop at a beer distributor's. A door opened, and a man stepped out and began guiding the driver as he backed up to the door. Presently, the man came over and shook my hand. I explained that I was the deceased man's daughter, and that I wanted to stay with him until he was really gone.

I expected a reaction at this, an, "Oh, no, dear, you don't want to do that!" What I got was a high school chemistry teacher with an enthusiasm for his subject. My father was about to become an object lesson.

Standing upright in the corner of this immaculately clean room, reminiscent of a garage except for two large wall ovens, was a big cardboard box. The two men put the box on a gurney and slid my father into it. Then they wheeled the gurney over to oven B and put him in, box and all. If there's been a viewing, the coffin is used. It would take about two and a half hours, at between seventeen hundred and two thousand degrees.

I noticed that there were two doors on the ovens. The outer one was solid and made of stainless steel. The other was a thick fire-brick door and had a small window; you could check the progress of the flames. There was a hole in the near end of the ceiling, over the chest cavity, where most of a person's organs are situated. The flame shot down out of that hole and began licking at the box my father was in.

I was a good student, curious, attentive, listening to the explanations about the air vent, how it's part of a system that works like a catalytic converter on a car; how the air circulates around the outside of the oven, and is cleansed of pollutants before it is released through the chimney. But then he started to lose me.

He—Crispini, I think his name was—was telling me stories about some of his experiences in the business. I heard them, but I didn't take them in. My mind wandered across the lawns of my childhood, my father pushing me on swings, carrying me around on his shoulders, laughing. I was often nervous when he laughed; I worried it wouldn't last. He had that infamous short fuse, my father. And he died the way he lived, suddenly, and in a burst of irritation. His heart gave out. It was as if a cloud passed over, and with it had come just one more change in mood.

I was looking at the little giftlike containers they put the ashes in when Mr. Crispini called out. "Come here," he said. "You might like to see what's going on."

Obediently, I walked over, without thinking about what I would see. The box was gone. The charred remnants of my father's skin were curling away in layers as they burned, like so many sheets of a newspaper. Some of the smaller pieces broke off and floated to the ceiling of the vault. And then, looking down my father's body, toward his legs, I saw something lift, like a long finger.

"Amazing, isn't it?" Crispini said, aware that I had pressed closer to the window. "Men get erections. I meant to warn you."

I should have been horrified. But I was fascinated. My father, always quite the ladies' man, would have loved it.

Later, when we rounded up the children and spread my father's ashes in the garden, I was struck by how all of our grand schemes fall victim to circumstances that have nothing to do with our wishes as we originally conceived them. My father had wanted to be beside my mother in the woods behind the house they built. Then he wanted to be beside his second wife on a hillside in California. And here we were, putting him in a garden that I don't believe he ever noticed.

We, too, had an idea once. We each wanted our ashes tossed into the Mediterranean, near Positano. That way, at least the one who was left to do it would get to go back to this wonderful place; there would be consolation, and peace, in that. The second one to die would leave that task to the children. It would be done in the same place, and in the same way.

But geography changes with our lives. I don't know now where I want my final place to be. What I can't get used to is that even when I do, it won't matter to you.

M A R C H   1 3

You would have loved to overhear the conversation Edward and I had on Saturday night after he ran into you and the new object of your affection at the liquor store.

Of all the times for me to decide to stay in the car—damn! I knew something was up by the way Edward bounced back into the driver's seat. He was practically licking his lips, savoring this coveted morsel like a well-fed crocodile. "You're going to be *sooo* sorry," he crooned, "that you didn't come in with me."

I got right to the point. "Is she pretty?" I asked,

wildly cursing myself for not helping him select the wine
that we were taking to dinner at Nina and Stephen's.

"Mm, yes, I'd say so," he replied thoughtfully.

Shit, I thought. "What kind of hair does she have?"
I asked, quickly adding, "Curly?," knowing he'd need
guidelines as to the content I was after. Men just don't
take in the right stuff, usually. A woman can walk into
a party, and within minutes she'll know who's there,
who's with whom, what they're wearing, and how everybody's getting along. Men can tell you how many
people were present.

In Edward's defense, I have to say that he's much
better than the average man. He'll tell you every single
detail about the food, right down to the kind of olive
oil that was used in the marinade for the roasted red
peppers. But I had my work cut out for me, given that
food was not the focal point here.

The answer to the curly question was, "Not really."
And the color, for your information, of your new love's
hair is brownish, grayish, blond. His inability to absorb
these simple details was maddening. I could forget about
the fine-tuning. I knew perfectly well that if our positions had been reversed, that is, if I had found myself
face-to-face with Pamela and a new boyfriend, I'd have
returned with a thicker portfolio, so to speak.

Edward couldn't even tell me how you were
dressed, whether it looked like an evening out, something really special, or whether you looked as if you
might be stopping in for wine before going back to her
place. He was equally useless on what she seemed to
think of running into Edward, your ex-wife's boy-

friend. I mean, it is possible to get a reading on these things, on whether, for instance, someone is indifferent—or not.

Now you might ask, as Nina has asked—loudly, I might add—what makes me think that who you're going out with is any of my business. When you seemed to be getting serious about Isabel, and I was full of objections (I thought Isabel was absolutely wrong for you), Nina said, "Just a minute, Emily. You can pick your first husband and you can pick your second husband, but you do *not* get to pick your first husband's second wife."

I don't know why not. Who's in a better position, after all, to determine the most appropriate mate for a man than the woman who lived with him for twenty years? Not that I'm going to be completely objective. As June said of Harvey's new girlfriend, "She's incredibly good-looking, and she makes a boatload of money. I just know she'll never make him happy."

No doubt June pictured Harvey with someone less glamorous, and more wholesome, which is to say heavier; someone, well, more his type. Women naturally prefer to be succeeded by "nice" and "down-to-earth," and perhaps a touch wide in the hips, as opposed to gorgeous.

It's not that I don't wish you well; I do. However, it's one thing for me to wish for your happiness and quite another to wish for it in quantities that exceed whatever we had at our happiest. It grieves me to think of you and your new love lazing in bed on Sunday mornings, looking up at a peeling ceiling that is one big water spot and planning the New Wing. (Incidentally, since the children are so much older now, don't you think that we should move the nursery to the guest wing?)

How I loved those times. They were not momentous; they were merely moments. But they were the links that connected us to each other in ways that were unique. Now they're in danger of being relegated to obscurity by the presence of strangers. Our past as each of us remembers it will bear us no witness.

All the more reason, then, that I should choose your new mate. Like me, she should be sensitive to the tug of history, which is to say she should be a woman of my age and perspective, someone with a past of her own, some gray hair, and a former husband whose uniqueness only she knows. Such a woman is more apt to appreciate the sanctity of those recollections than someone younger, whose history has yet to occur.

I keep thinking about the woman Edward saw in the liquor store—the one with the not-really-curly, brownish, grayish, blond hair. I think of her and I imagine Harvey or June coming to me one day and saying, "She's perfect—the woman he should have married in the first place."

Forgive my proprietary interest, but I can think of somebody better. What's wrong with the woman you should have married in the second place?

To My Ex-Husband

It could only happen to Harvey. The day that he came to give us the news will live on in my memory as one of the more telling episodes of Harvey's life, at once awful and hilarious. I was dying to talk to you about it then, but no one was to know. "You can't say a *thing*," Harvey had said. I knew, though, that he'd probably been saying that to all his best friends. Harvey can't keep a secret, even—probably most especially—his own.

Now, since the word is officially out, I can share the story with someone who'd appreciate it. He came by on a Saturday a few weeks ago, and before I could say hello, he was racing around the house, breathlessly closing all the doors so that he wouldn't be overheard. It was a move that made sense, considering that my house often has the appearance of a youth hostel these days. But spring break was over, Tony was back at school, and Melissa was spending the weekend with a friend. I explained this, but he continued sealing us off room by room. Finally, when there was no place to go but into the kitchen closet, he sat down and said, "You won't believe this."

"I'll believe it," I said, which was true, because only unbelievable things happen to Harvey. He makes the unbelievable completely believable.

"Meg is pregnant," he said.

"I don't believe it," I said, and sat down.

Just then Edward came home, walking into an atmosphere of stunned silence.

"What's up?" he said, after a quick glance at Harvey, who was wearing his wide-eyed, I've-really-done-it-this-time expression. Edward didn't believe it either, not that Meg was pregnant, but that Harvey was going to get married.

"*Married!*" Edward said. "People don't have to get married anymore, especially not fifty-year-old people."

Then Harvey told us about the tests he was having, to rule out cancer. He thought he had an ulcer.

"Harvey," Edward said, with a black cackle. "You're the only guy I know for whom cancer could be construed as a solution. The bad news: Meg's pregnant. The good news: You only have twenty-four hours to live."

Well, as I said, it could only happen to Harvey. Meg is going to have the baby, period. She doesn't want Jamie to be an only child and, at thirty-eight, she's getting short on time. Harvey's feeling is that he can't not be part of it. So there you are. He probably would have gotten married anyway because he loves Meg, but he would never have *decided* to get married. Harvey doesn't decide things. Fate decides. Well, fate has made some good decisions, ultimately. I hope it does as well with his divorce. Harvey isn't sure if anyone has filed yet.

p.s. Everyone tells me that the woman in your life—Linda?—is "really nice." Harvey apparently thought I was strong enough for him to add "cute."

To My Ex-Husband

I keep waiting for things to change between us, but they never do. Maybe the trouble is that I'm not waiting; I'm expecting.

I'm not sure which is worse—that you couldn't be happy for me, or that you couldn't pretend to be. I suppose, given the choice, I'd rather have the truth, but it doesn't exactly facilitate the occasion. You seem so much happier now yourself—the house, Linda—that I thought you could afford to be more generous, more gracious. Edward says that in Italian there's an expression, *"ti auguro ogni bene,"* for which there is no exact English equivalent, but it means, I wish the best for you. It hurts me to see that you can't wish the best for me, that this is what it's come to, even when your life is going well.

Which brings me to what I believe has been at the core of so much of my frustration with you: You don't want me to perceive you as happier. Whenever things work out for you, whenever there's the smallest ray of sunshine seeping in under the window shade, you're quick to point out how slight that ray really is, and that just behind it all is dark and hopeless. It's true you've bought a house; it's nice, but I'm given to believe that it hasn't changed anything. You're still alone. You still miss your family. You're seeing someone named Linda, yes, but you're seeing a lot of people. You say that for you, there's only one marriage in life, one person. Every other woman seems wrong somehow, an affair. You've forgotten that at one time you didn't seem to have any problem with that.

There's nothing so terribly wrong, I guess, in being determined to be miserable. But I do think there might be something wrong in using it the way you have used it—to make me feel guilty, to diminish whatever pleasure I might have. You said once, in Dr. Block's office, when you were apologizing for all the "bad" things that you had done, that you knew that you had been the agent of pain, not just for me, but for Annie and Peter. I wore the effect on my face; it moved you.

I feel that way now. I avert my eyes so that I won't be brought in. Your unwillingness to let go and move on is a hook you hold out at arm's length to snag me in my path.

You remind me of a child whose mother has left him at camp to have a good time and who, in spite of himself, has a good time. He learns to swim and play dodge ball. He makes friends. His misery is something he forgets. But when he comes home, there is reproach in his every look, every gesture. His mother has left him, and now the payment is due.

There was a time when I was furious about all this, especially when your vulnerability had so much power. Everybody bent over backward to protect you. The kids didn't mention my name in your presence; I was careful never to say "we" when I talked to you, as if Edward didn't exist. I didn't want him to pick me up at the airport after Annie's graduation because I didn't want to run the risk that you would see him. It was enough for you to be in your shoes. Why did I have to be in there, too?

Then, one morning, Dr. Bloom asked me whether it would help if I knew that, for whatever neurotic reason, you couldn't do better. "Couldn't?" I had thought the word was "wouldn't."

And with that Dr. Bloom deprived me of much of my reason for being angry. I didn't like giving my anger up. It had given me my energy; it had served me. But it was a habit, like smoking. What am I going to do instead, I wondered; what's going to make me interesting? I didn't have any idea, but it would be fun finding out.

JUNE 6

I wasn't going to tell you this; I wasn't going to tell anyone. But now, since I've told everyone, it only seems fair that I should tell you, too. Besides, I want to keep the record straight and this isn't the time to start omitting things.

Edward and I were nearing the end of a bottle of zinfandel on Saturday night when I mentioned to him that you were having Linda and Annie to dinner so that you could introduce them. (Bear in mind that, although I'd heard a lot of nice things about Linda, I'd never actually seen her, and Edward wasn't much help in filling me in.)

Edward listened, staring thoughtfully into his wine and twirling the stem of his glass between his fingers. "What exactly did you have in mind?" he asked.

"Oh, nothing," I said. "Just that I'd love to go peek in the windows."

"Well, what are we waiting for?" he said, putting down his glass and reaching for the car keys. I couldn't believe it, a man who would indulge my mischievousness, my naughtiness. But then, as I was beginning to discover, Edward himself is naughty. *Incredible,* I thought. A naughty dentist. The man was full of surprises.

A few minutes later, we were walking up your street, trying to stay within the shadows of the trees. Edward was completely cool, as though we spied on our former spouses every evening, but I was both giddy and terrified. I thought that I might wet my pants.

We sped up the front walk, and then around to the side of the house and into the sticker bushes. (You might be gratified to know that we were both wearing shorts.) I'd had no idea how high the dining-room windows were. Even standing on our toes and gripping the window ledge by our fingertips, we could barely see into the room. The big problem, though, was that you were sitting with your back to the window, and it was almost impossible to see Linda, except for a corner of her hair.

Occasionally you would reach for something, and I could see some of her face. She seemed nervous. And Harvey was right. Linda was cute.

"What do you think they're eating?" Edward whispered. "It looks like some kind of chops." The food— of course. The real reason for his mission. Just then you got up from the table and moved toward the front door.

"He's coming!" Edward said, grabbing my hand and pulling me through the bushes. We ran toward the gate to the backyard, but we couldn't get it open. There was absolutely nowhere to go. I started giggling uncontrollably, so Edward pressed his hand over my mouth, which made me laugh all the more.

You never did come outside, as far as we know. We waited until we thought the coast was clear, then made our way back to the car. Edward walked; I ran. As we drove away, he said, "Didn't anyone ever tell you not to run from the scene of a crime?"

The scars of my indiscretion are still with me. My legs look as if I'd been attacked by a raccoon. Edward's probably do, too, but his shame is concealed by a manly carpet of hair.

I'm glad you didn't catch us; it would have been awfully embarrassing. Much more fun, too, to tell the story myself, as one who'd escaped, than to think that anyone would hear about it from your perspective, as the captor: "I found my ex-wife and her fiancé peering through my dining-room window the other night . . . how *perfectly* appalling. God knows what Linda must have thought . . ."

God knows what Annie would think; but then, I've never impressed Annie as a model of decorum. I'm a woman, remember, who is known to have climbed over a construction barrier and sink into eighteen inches of freshly poured concrete because she was too lazy to walk around the block. Children form an early opinion of their mother when construction workers whistle, and people in traffic jams yell out the windows of their cars, "Whatdja think it was, lady, a Chinese restaurant?"

Annie's always been so much more of a grown-up than I. Do you recall what she said that time I had my hair cut by that sadist who called himself an artist? "Oh, Mommy, why do you do these things?"

A sensible person might ask. But I expect I'll go on doing them until I die.

JULY 14

Nina and I have been having nuptial talks. It was she who got me into this, so I'm holding her responsible for easing my every anxiety. She started working on me a year ago, when she was doing a review of Jake's. I had just ordered the grilled chicken sandwich—she was having the tuna steak and a side dish of string sweet potato fries—when she said, "Emily, you just have to marry this man, that's all there is to it."

These were disquieting words to the waiter, who had just returned with our iced tea and thought she was talking about him; but one of us is always saying something disquieting. Just the week before, in a crowded outdoor cafe, Nina had asked me what my hairdresser charged for a haircut. "Forty dollars for a cut," I said, "and five dollars extra for a blow job. Uh, *dry*," I added quickly, but it was too late. Nina was on her way under the table.

Anyway, I don't often argue with Nina; you know that. I tend to go along with her because she usually manages to convince me that hers is the only reasonable view. Almost invariably, she turns out to be right, a notable exception being the time she encouraged me to get a boarder and Valerie came to live with me.

So that day at Jake's she was telling me I had to get married. I loved the vintage, old-timey quality of the phrase, calling forth the hasty selection of crystal and silver patterns. But she was thinking, actually, of health insurance. As someone who spends thousands of dollars a year on yeast treatments and other related ailments, I got her point. I had nothing against a good insurance plan, but my relationship with Edward had been a romance. Romance and marriage, as so many of us had learned, were two quite different things.

When you're in love, you overlook annoyances. When you're in love, the way his teeth clink on the spoon each time he takes a mouthful of soup isn't something you really notice. But get married, and that noise will punctuate your sentences. It will be the conversational equivalent of water torture.

You and I had been married for twenty years—not forever, I grant you. But two decades is nothing to write off. Would I want to be married to Edward in twenty years? In twenty years he will be sixty-eight, an old man. Would I want to marry someone who's going to be an old man?

And what about me? What went through Edward's mind as, each morning, I stirred a hefty teaspoon of Fiberall into a glass of orange juice? More and more of what went into my mouth each year was for medicinal purposes. I was waiting for the all-fiber fettucine, and then I'd be set.

Otherwise, I wanted everything to stay as it was. There were days, it was true, when I hoped Melissa would leave for school in the morning and run away and get married in the afternoon. I was too old for the habits of adolescents, too old for sulking and door-slamming. But Edward was the indispensable part of the package. No matter what was going on, even when we were arguing about Melissa, which was often, even if I was having menstrual cramps and was bloated, even if he was paying entirely too much attention to those fish, I craved him with a passion I had not thought possible in me. The relationship was not about children, though we had them and loved them and took care of them when they were here; the relationship was about us. We were not starting a family; we had none of the plans that younger couples do. There were no peripherals. We were not asking ourselves, What will the future hold, what will we be? We already knew.

The point was to be together, to revel in what we had to offer each other. I just didn't see how being married was going to add anything. On the contrary, I thought marriage would subtract.

Nor had it escaped me that the success rate for second marriages was none too encouraging. One had a better chance of staying married the first time. Maybe that was because once you learn that you can get divorced and the sky won't fall, you can do it again. The first divorce is like the first murder; you've already got blood on your hands.

But I didn't want to get divorced again, not ever. And if I didn't get married again, I wouldn't have to worry about it. That was my guarantee.

Each day Edward lived here with me was by choice. He could leave at any time. At any time, I could ask him to leave. We were not stuck by contract. All the same, a time came when I started to change. Without realizing what was happening, I lowered my resistance. I started wondering if what I thought was choice, what I called not being stuck, was more like having one foot out the door. What had sounded like an option had all the earmarks of an escape hatch. So here I was, at lunch with Nina and having a nuptial talk. Maybe she had scared me about the insurance, I didn't know. But I was getting excited. I felt different. "Commitment" seems like such a simple, overused word. But if that was it, if that was the thing that was making it different, then I was suddenly, wholeheartedly, all for it.

The only thing I hadn't squared with myself was the extent to which I was going to bring my first husband into my second marriage. We were at Odeon, and Nina was concentrating on the pork medallions in some kind of thick, dark, brown sauce. I had the premarital jitters and could have been eating anything. I mean that literally—anything and everything. Other people who have premarital jitters eat nothing. My appetite was affected only to the extent that I was indiscriminate.

I took a forkful of something that may have been a breast of duck and said I would always think of Edward as my lover, not my husband. She nodded and said something that sounded like "piquant." Hand it to Nina, the consummate professional.

I don't know how she does it, week after week. This may sound incredible coming from me, but I don't know if I could earn my living by eating. Once it became work, I don't think I could do it anymore. Nina, on the other hand, is always sharp, always concentrating. She never takes anything for granted. I've known restaurant reviewers in this city who chain-smoked or drank or both. They made or broke the reputations of restaurants on their impressions of food they could not possibly taste. I admired Nina tremendously, but I could hardly get her attention.

"You know," I said, "if Edward and Nick were each about to drop off the edge of the world, and I could only save one of them, I would save Nick." She looked up from her plate.

"You," she said, "are retarded."

I smiled, though she wasn't kidding. She means everything she says. I thought of Stephen, sweet, gentle Stephen, with his fatherly good nature and his innate sense of right; he can be funny, but, unlike Nina, never acerbic. "Oh, Nina, you don't mean that," he'll say.

"But I do mean it," she'll reply. He never believes her, of course.

I told Nina that I didn't really feel that way any-more, but that until very recently I had. I loved Edward; but I needed you in the world with me. I couldn't be the only one who would remember the children when they were newborns, their first words, the way they sounded when they talked. It was too huge a responsibility. Even now I look at a picture of Annie at two, and I hear you imitating her froggy little voice.

I didn't go into all this with Nina. I didn't bother explaining, because Nina wouldn't have understood how confusing those feelings had been. I had them at a time when I was looking for perfect clarity. What changed was not my vision so much, but my willingness to live with ambivalence.

To My Ex-Husband

JULY 26

So once again Harvey has done the unbelievable. Or maybe Meg has; I'm not up on the gene stuff. Anyway, I don't believe it. *Twins.* A boy and a girl, according to the amniocentesis. There is a reason, after all, why I see Harvey's life as a Shakespearean comedy. I asked him if he was going to name them Sebastian and Viola, as in *Twelfth Night.* He wasn't amused. "I thought I was having this second little family," he said. "Instead, I'm having a farce."

Fate has again fallen right into Harvey's hands and given him great material. He'll pretend to be miserable, and we will all love to hear about it. But while we're laughing, we will know that secretly he's thrilled.

AUGUST 8

My mother is too much. This morning, a UPS truck pulled up with a big box from Florida. It was a silk negligee and a matching robe. And there was this subtle aspect—it was ivory rather than white. My mother has put her semi-seal of approval on my sins. She sure has mellowed! But, unfortunately, my marriage plans have made her somewhat self-conscious. When I called to thank her, she asked if it bothered me that she was not planning to get married.

"Emily," she said cautiously, "this way Fred and I have a little more money."

Hard to believe that this was my mother talking, hard to believe that she and Fred actually sat down and said, "Oh, let's not get married; let's just collect these two social security checks."

Everybody calls her Mrs. Graham, anyway. Just as everybody will no doubt call me Mrs. Ventura, though I'm not taking Edward's name. My students are so disappointed. They love change. It's romantic. One of the girls said, "But Mrs. Moore, why get married if you're not going to change your name?"

My God. What do you say to that?

But I can't be changing my name at this age. Nor, if it's of any interest to you, will Dickens. He is, and has always been, Dickens Moore, though he will enjoy a new and interesting status officially as Edward's stepdog.

When you and I were divorced, I'd have given up Moore and taken my maiden name back, but for two reasons. First, it's hard enough to get recognition as a writer without changing your name. And I'm not going to graft a new name onto an old name with the help of a hyphen. People are madly, joyously, hyphenating— until, in disillusion, they unhyphenate. Say Pearl Rudenke, the loan officer in your bank, gets married and becomes Pearl Rudenke-Betterbed. Then she gets divorced, and remarried. She calls herself Pearl Betterbed-Thames. Next thing, you know, she's refusing to lend you money as plain old Pearl Betterbed. So fickle. You begin to think that maybe it was a marriage in hyphen only.

The second reason I'm not snatching back my maiden name is one you already know. I hated Massengill. I always felt so fortunate to marry someone whose name was simple and pure and without pharmaceutical overtones. "There's no connection," my mother felt compelled to explain time and again. Of course, not everyone is so hygienically inclined as to have made the connection, so they had to ask.

"Well, those douche things," she would say, trying to sound offhand. As a teenager, this infuriated me. Why couldn't she just shut up? Douches went into vaginas. Vaginas had to do with sex. Why did my mother have to be talking about sex?

By and by, I saw that my mother was exercising her naughty side. Rebellion was so much more tasteful once upon a time, wasn't it?

Now here she is, sending her daughter a decidedly tasteful but nevertheless overtly sensual gift on the occasion of her second marriage. I'm incredibly touched at how supportive my mother has been. I don't know if she blamed me for what happened to us. I thought so at first. Her impulse has always been to assume that I'm at fault. And mine, in turn, has been to believe that she was right. She wasn't one who took a philosophical view, as my father did. She never considered that things had a way of working out for the best, especially if I had anything to do with them.

Lately, though, she seems to have become so much more accepting of a larger, not to say divine, scheme, something outside herself, beyond her control. She sees that I'm happy. And maybe, for the first time in my life, that's all she's asking.

I wonder if you remember, when he was about seven, Peter's wanting to know why my mother and